$16 U.S.

TWIST

Also by Simon Lane

Le Veilleur

Still-Life With Books

Fear

Boca a Boca

The Real Illusion

TWIST

a novel
by

SIMON LANE

ABINGDON SQUARE PUBLISHING
New York

Design: Abingdon Square Publishing

TWIST

is published by
Abingdon Square Publishing Ltd.
463 West Street, Suite G122
New York, NY 10014
www.abingdonsquarepublishing.com

ISBN 978-0-9823480-5-5
Library of Congress Control Number: 2010932260

First printing: September 2010
Printed in the United States of America

For Betsy

CONTENTS

"I scáth a chéile a mhaireann na daoine."
Proverb

"Ah, penny, brown penny, brown penny,
I am looped in the loops of her hair."
WB Yeats

Part One

I

1

300. Has a nice ring to it. Two rings, in fact. They are like eyes. You could look through them if you wished. Look into the future, look into the past, look wherever you wanted.

Just now, I found myself wondering what I would do with them. With the rings. I could get twin tigers to jump through them; once I had set them on fire, that is. I could turn them into tunnels, one heading east, one heading west, and have the traffic of ages pass through them, so that the audience becomes mesmerised, just as we were once mesmerised, seated in the front row of the *Cirque du Nord*, when real tigers bowed at our feet.

I could turn them around, transforming them into binoculars (twins, the French call them, in the feminine) so that time and tide disappear, submerged by one of myriad details selected at random, such as the time the other half stole the girl I was with after I passed out on the floor of the Rally. Yes, I will invert them, put my eyes to their cold rims and transport myself backwards through time, turn them on my past, so that all becomes clear and obvious. Look, boys! I'm travelling at the speed of noughts!

Or I'll do nothing with them. I'll ignore them, allow them to drift in the air around me, leave them as words slipping in one ear, out the other. Three hundred.

I bring my hands to my face and peer through my fingers, as I did long ago, as a child, pretending not to cheat on the brothers. Now, everything becomes clear to me. I am no longer enclosed, I am looking out through the thick light of day, I can feel the wind as it flies over the waves and whips the side of my face. I have one arm around Elska, the other grasps her by the elbow; the sky is blue, deep blue, the sea is dark, almost black, there is a line of land, green-topped cliffs behind us, and the ship rolls in the swell as the stranger before us grapples with the cheap box camera I have just handed him. The disposable object meets the disposable instant.

"Immortalise us, stranger! Don't worry about the edges!"

Agostini is always talking about the edges. He says that is what photography is all about. Getting the edges right. Agostini is right about many things and he must know what he is talking about when it comes to photography because he makes an awful lot of money out of it.

"It's not like life, Twist. You have to get everything right. When you look through the viewfinder, you have to check the edges. You can have a great subject and have captured it well, but it has to be perfectly composed otherwise it's no good."

"I don't care much for edges, Agostini."

"It's true, Twist. What I'm saying. Not important. But true. Even if it's not like life."

"Come off it, Agostini!"

I am looking at the world with new eyes. New noughts. I see everything laid out, organised, orchestrated, as if for me and for me alone. This world exists and will always exist, whatever happens; it is fixed in my mind like a photograph, not necessarily the one of me and Elska, perhaps one of the ones, in black and white, which used to sit on the piano, of me and the other half, or of the mammy and Dad. Or of the five of us, for there was once an elder brother, who joined the Legion for no other reason than that he didn't know what else to do with himself. "Stick to poetry, like Dad," we told him. "Better than getting yourself killed in the bloody army." Which is exactly what he did, blown up defusing an anti-personnel mine in Chad. The mammy never got over it. Why should she have done? She's dead too and her soul is back in Ireland, where it belongs. She's smiling in the photograph. She was always smiling, even when things were bad. But she didn't smile much when Myles fell off the branch.

I think there's a medal somewhere. *Dulce et decorum est.* And a poem I can't read, not because it's bad, which it is, but because Myles talks about love as if it belonged to someone else. Could he have been so lonely? I'll ask him later. He was good to us and I'd have given him a medal every day of the week if I could have afforded it.

Whatever was good or bad, this world came to me as a blessing and a malediction and I always accepted it as such. I can see it now, set in motion as if it were a child's globe I had flicked with my index finger. This orb still turns, it will never stop turning, not until the day when another mass of metal and mineral collides with it. It was born from chaos, from an act of violence, and it will end its days and nights thus. As it spins, I close my eyes again and then place my finger upon it. I smile and set the orb in motion again, picking it up so that it perfectly balances on my finger. And then I toss it into the air, watching it dance upon the wind before finally disappearing over the horizon. The day passes, the year turns oblivion full circle. And here I am, a nondescript particle, lost somewhere within the emptiness. Alone in a crowded space, insulated from all that I have known, I achieve extinction, an outsider hovering on the periphery of existence, and I know that after all this, after Paris and Elska and Agostini's Edges, I will only come alive again after I have sat down with the other half and taken that first draught of stout, for what can compare to a memory slowly poured? The past is an open book and nothing is certain and sure-fired, as Holy God used to say to us when we were little, our hands reaching up to the counter.

The noughts change all of a sudden, all on their own, from two eyes to two heads, meeting within the neatly reversed concavity of a silver spoon, twin reflections moving forwards for the benefit of the camera to take up the whole screen, crowding out the details of a lunchtime at Swallows'. We raise our tankards. This is the moment! I now propose the toast and present the other half with the birthday poem, which came to me, in a cloudlet, as I stepped out from the Alabama this morning and which, for surprise purposes, I'll have to keep a secret.

2

I met Elska at a party, which is not strictly true, as I had met her before. In fact, I knew her without knowing her. We saw each other but never spoke, it was an oblique sort of friendship, conducted at a distance, more animal than human. Like tigers, perhaps. Afterwards, we would say that our thoughts corresponded, that there was something telepathic about those earlier times which needed no explanation and which made the future, now past, inevitable. Telepathic? Why ever not? There is no essential mystery to life, life being essentially mysterious.

I met her again, yet truly for the first time, at a party, is a fairer way of putting it, of looking through the noughts. Even then we didn't speak much, but we registered each other in a new way and that, for me at least, was enough. It was in Paris, of course, where everything important in my life has happened at one time or another, home away from home, city of flight.

I had been away in New York, on Long Island, for a year. Fishing, mostly. Bonito, blue fish, bass, the occasional mako shark, which we – Mad Joe and I – would marinate in ginger and soy sauce and then barbecue. We were always looking for tuna, but we never got one. Mad Joe said he'd once seen a tuna with eyes the size of car headlamps and I can never get that out of my mind, every time I cross the street I think I'm going to get run over by one, a great big tuna weaving its way through the traffic and heading straight towards me.

Hemingway's fictional son, or real son, in one of his books, nearly catches a thousand-pound swordfish. Yes, there are monsters out there, imagined and otherwise, and it is possible to catch them if you make enough luck for yourself. I didn't manage it, but I worked as mate for a while on a charter boat which took care of a few months, allowing me to lose myself to a world of fresh and quiet emptiness and to dream of one day catching my own monster. My world belongs to another constellation, within which the sound of the sea is rarely heard, the knock of salt beats far from the heart; there are no fish, only people, memories, drinks to be had, arguments with a tired reflection, mischief and laughter, but I sometimes escape it, when I feel my time full. I have been told we come from the sea, or near it, the family, the species, all from the sea, cast up by a freak wave and landed, wet and flapping. The mammy hailed from Brunmore and we all went there, once, together; the days were soft and Myles trod on an urchin.

I have done many things and yet I have done nothing. No matter. It was the way I was taught to be. It was always the present with us, with the O'Learys. "Keep it all going in the now direction," said Dad. "That way you'll know where you are."

I always thought that any meaning to be derived from life lay in the simple fact of existence – breathing, laughing – as Dad had explained. I am no fatalist, yet I usually permit my destiny to fall in my lap, rather than pursuing it with a rod or a rifle, reeling it in from the depths or felling it with a bullet. Except for the tuna, that is. That's different. The time for that will come if I make it come, for time is never borrowed, only stolen. As for Dad, how curious that a man who devoted his life to dreaming so much should have appeared, on the face of it, so pragmatic. Such is the nature of the poet, however, a contradiction, an enigma, the resolution of opposing forces through inexplicable harmonies of language and meaning.

Luck is made. We all knew that. One night, last winter, I recited a poem Dad wrote years ago, called "Heaven and Hell", to a man in a blue suit with a ponytail at the Crest Hotel in Sag Harbor. The man bought me a drink. To my astonishment, he offered to buy the poem.

"You can't buy a poem, Mister. It's not a bean or a bottle."

He was a pop star, or a producer, and, because everything can be bought in America, he bought it. "Fine," said I. "But you're not buying the poem without a lawyer present." So, I got one and we made the transaction.

A few months later, the lawyer called me and said that the poem had been turned into a song, which had become a hit record and, if I wished, I could listen to it on the wireless. "To hell with the wireless, what about the money?" I said. It turned out that my percentage had become two hundred thousand dollars.

That was a year ago, almost to the day. I was rich. So, I came back to Paris and checked in to the old Alabama, on the rue de Seine. Room 76. I had a year of living to do without worrying about money. Dad was dead, and the mammy, and Myles, there was only the other half, in London. I had wired him fifty per cent of the profit to make it all even, so there I was, with the readies, clean and clean-shaven, a new man, as it were, foot-free and fancy-less.

The Alabama is a special place and the owner, Max, and Dad were already friends before we were born. Dad used to take us there and we would sit in the foyer, listening to what he and Max had to say. Max respected Dad and thought he was a fine poet, although Max liked Byron and Dad couldn't stand the man. "Just another English twit," he would say and Max would laugh because he didn't care either way and he knew Dad didn't.

Perhaps this was what they had in common, their ambivalence. It was a sham, of course, but people can turn a sham into a way of life without much effort, hiding what they really think and feel for as long as they wish. It is a quality that makes all of us actors, some good, some bad, but actors all the same. As for Max, he is long gone but I often feel his presence as I get into the lift: a burst of laughter, a pinch of sherbet, a button pushed to infancy.

As soon as I got back to Paris, I ran into Agostini and it was Agostini who told me about the party. Everyone would be there, he said.

"So, what's it like to be back, Twist?" asked Agostini, as we walked from the Rally towards the river in the still, summer twilight.

"I'm never away. That's what it's like."

"What are you going to do?"

"You always ask me that, Agostini. Nothing. This, for the time being."

"Your friend, Moraes, is in town. He'll be at the party."

"Good. I'm glad there'll be some uprights to laugh with. What about you, Agostini? Met any pretty girls lately trying to be equal or superior?"

"Me? I don't change."

"No one changes, Agostini. That's the whole point."

"That's where you're wrong, Twist. Love can change you. If you want it to. If you allow it to. But then, you never fall in love, do you?"

"I'm not averse to the idea. But it's true I don't give it much thought."

"It's not something you think about. It's something that happens."

3

300. The speed of noughts. Leading to Elska. Elska always rose above everything, never more so than at that party. It was a secret, her aloofness, her distance, not just the existence of it but the way she managed to convey it, like a poem she had once composed for herself.

Understanding the poem was the key to her personality, the first step inside a labyrinth. Within it could be found many hopefuls, quite lost, floundering, not knowing which way to turn. One did not necessarily help such unfortunates, one ignored them and pressed on, thread in hand, so as to discover the real secret, which was her love. As for those *cognoscenti* who might have succeeded in getting near the heart of the matter, one simply hoodwinked them by giving them false directions. You had to keep your wits about you with Elska.

Her luminous blue eyes, the wryness of that smile and the sound of her laughter, infectious and rhetorical, all these things immediately distinguished her, as if she were the only person in the room. That evening she wore a simple cocktail dress and no make-up, not a trace of it, and her dark, almost black hair was tied back with a silver clip that occasionally caught the light as she turned to one side or the other, to listen or to look around. She was fairly tall, but not too tall. And she had had the first two centimetres of her fringe dyed green, for some reason.

Elska always listened. And observed. She never put a foot wrong and this was her elegance, or part of it. There was also her way of moving, almost imperceptibly, so that she somehow became omnipresent. Her all-seeing eye, her interrogatory gaze, the overt charm of her smile, especially when understated, constituted a spell from which few people seemed able, or willing, to extricate themselves.

I was caught, from the moment I saw her again, even from the safe distance of a dozen others, whose heads, clumsy gestures and drinking hands, moving in rhythm to music heard or imagined, would part, as if in unison, allowing me another glimpse of her, and still another. Even then I felt almost paralysed, unable to approach because I was afraid, not of her, but of myself, haunted by Agostini's words to me about love and wondering why it was I could never take a woman seriously. Well, here was a woman to take seriously. She was standing in the same room as me; and I didn't even have to go through the bother of introducing myself.

Agostini was right about one thing: everyone was there. Except Moraes, of course. I tried to distract myself, but all I could think of was Elska. An American painter told me about the press he had received for his recent exhibition before telling me in some detail about the next one. Then a Frenchman with a lisp asked me about Dad. Was it true or not true that he had been a friend of Beckett? Finally, Moraes arrived. We stood in a corner and had a drink.

"She's over there, Moraes."

"Who?"

"Elska. So, who is she with? She must be with someone. How could she not be?"

"She's married now, Twist."

"Married?"

"Yes. Married."

"When?" I was stunned.

"About a year ago. Maybe longer."

"And to who? To whom?"

"Flyte."

"Flyte?"

"Isn't he a friend of yours?"

"Of course. I'm just out of touch, that's all. I've only been back in Paris a couple of days."

"And you've fallen for her?"

"How did you guess?"

"But watch out. You're not used to falling in love. *Passarinho que come pedra sabe o cu que tem.*"

A girl had appeared to interrupt us. She took Moraes by the arm and steered him towards a small group on the other side of the room.

I called after him. "What's a *passarinho*?"

"Tell you later!" came the reply, over his shoulder.

I stood alone for a while, looking at everyone and telling myself that nothing had changed, that my year away might just as well have been five minutes, time to leave the party and rejoin it. Elska stayed where she was. I could tell she had seen me. At one point, she smiled at me. Agostini reappeared, drunk, with a blonde on his arm who giggled and said she was an actress. All of a sudden, Elska was standing amongst us.

"Hello, Agostini," she said, softly.

"Hello, Elska. This is Marie, I think. And this is…"

"I know who this is. How are you, Twist?"

"I'm fine, Elska. Just fine."

"You don't look older."

"Neither do you. Got yourself an emerald fringe. Looks good, too."

"I'm not sure it's emerald."

"Perhaps it's indefinable. Colours don't actually exist, do they? I mean, they change all the time."

Someone else had appeared and, before I knew it, had taken Elska away from me. He was shorter than she was and they looked perfectly incongruous as they vanished in the crowd.

"So who was that, Agostini? Where's Flyte?"

"Flyte? I don't think he's here."

"There I was, having a chat. And then she's gone, abducted by a dwarf. Where's he taken her? His cave?"

I stayed all night at the party and we were still drinking cocktails at dawn. But I didn't see Elska again. Eventually, I said good-bye and left. I found myself walking back over the river to the Left Bank with a woman who might have been Russian, or Polish. She had a sharp, piercing laugh, which I can still hear ringing in my ears as we divide the landscape. Her face was smeared with lipstick; even though she stepped with great deliberation to compensate for her drunkenness, she managed to get one of her high heels stuck in the pavement grille outside the Café de Flore. Paris was coming to life and the streets were being cleaned. They were still warm, despite the hour. The woman began to laugh hysterically so I asked one of the street cleaners to hose her down. Afterwards, I extracted her shoe from the grille and we sat down on the terrace for coffee. The waiter called Patrick brought the woman a towel and she dried herself off. Then Patrick brought two glasses of champagne and offered them to us on the house. The woman forgave me and I laughed with her as we looked at Paris awakening. We parted at the rue Bonaparte and I never saw her again.

4

Everything spins away in the slipstream. What did Durrell say? *"A city becomes a world when one loves one of its inhabitants."* Well, I always loved Paris, with or without a woman. We were born there, after all.

As for Elska, I feel the matter unfinished, even though we are safely apart, divided, and shall doubtless remain thus. Everything has come full circle and I am caught upon the circumference somewhere near the top, not knowing where I am in time and space, just turning idly through the past, the future, the present. This is the circle that turns before and after Elska, it contains the eternity pressing upon my existence. Dad once spoke of it:

"'Tween the fore and after/'Twixt the leer and laughter."

Our last moments, yesterday, have become a neat enough coda to the whole thing, yet oddly unsatisfying, as if there could have been more, so much more, to go on. I was acting too much; I should have said what was really in my heart, but pride blocked it. And Elska wanted to make some form of resumé, a closing speech. Was she trying to justify herself? I doubt it.

"You're hopeless, Twist. Hopeless. You think you have nothing to lose. But you're wrong."

Everything is so illusory and equivocal. So why does it bother me? Have I turned her into something more important than she is because I can't have her, because I won't see her again? We always want what we can't have. Can it really be that simple? One still has to consider that part of the equation and equalize it in order to establish the truth, however. A truth, at least.

We are travelling at maximum speed, the landscape is a moving picture, yet we are immobile, we who slip through it. Only the smoke from our cigarettes proves that we are alive. The luggage which is our collective memory, packed in disorder, hangs over our heads like a threat, meeting in the inevitable collision of imminent forces. The disorder, like all things, is noted by default for, while it will ultimately lead to its antithesis, we all know the inverse to be true, that only from order will we encounter the mysterious, enchanting joys of chaos. Chaos! An act of faith, through which all art flows, and all of life, overpowering, exquisite, imponderable and sublime in its uselessness!

We are all of us, me and countless strangers, escaping, and even if the speed which binds us is an illusion, it nevertheless becomes a part of us, a part of our being, tainting all that we do, so that every act is one held in suspension, to be examined by anyone wishing and able to observe it. A complicity soon results from this haphazard union of disparate souls, one which accords with our apparently shared objective, to reach a destination at a fixed time, with or without mishap, even if the destination seems somehow insignificant as we sit here caught in the moment.

London? Strange trajectory, foreign, familiar, symbol more than anything else. Home of the other half. The restaurant, Swallows', next to the publisher, where Dad used to take us every birthday on the boat train. The Channel, heaving sea, white cliffs. The station, not a battle then but a queen. The cab with the fold-down seats, the waiting in an empty office, me, the other half, Myles, arguing the merits of Yeats, skirts, beer. All gone, forever, and Dad, too. Not like Myles. Blew himself up but in a different way, with a bottle. So, there's just me and the other half, meeting today for a reunion of the three tenses, for he'll be sure to ask where I'm headed and I'll tell him I want to lie in a hammock and sleep it all off. What was he called, Dad's editor? Towne? Browne?

"Your father's a great writer, boys. As good as anyone. Better. But he drinks too much."

Suppose he's dead, too. He was already old then. But everyone's already old when you're young. When he asked us if we were going to be writers, Myles told him one should never try to follow in the footsteps. He laughed as if he understood. But he didn't. Whatever his name was. Dad didn't dislike him, though. "He's thorough, no harm in that, boys," he said to us once, as we sat down for the fish and *frites*.

Is there a doctor on board this train?

Of course, I cannot tell whether those around me, visible or not, are escaping, as I am escaping. Frankly, it is of little concern to me. The sadness or regret expressed in a glance or downturned expression may touch me, but not now, for I am busy with my thoughts, arranging them, planning them, controlling them; and with myself, seeking a position of comfort and stability, just as one places a fresh piece of paper onto a horizontal surface and aligns one pen, or pencil, beside it, the better to embark upon that task known to be exclusive, solitary and irrevocable. I have been told things come easily to me. Well, let's see how difficult I can make it.

We are travelling at maximum speed! Three hundred kilometres per hour!

Strange: you always feel you are doing something worthwhile when you're travelling fast. And, when you're travelling at maximum speed, it's practically a catharsis. Yet I still don't really know why I'm doing this: writing, for the first time, that is. Ford Madox Ford began *The Good Soldier* on his fortieth birthday. He said it was a good moment to set things down. He wanted to call it *The Saddest Story*, but they wouldn't let him. There must have been a Browne somewhere. Or a Towne. Dad loved that book, which might surprise some people. He gave me a copy of it once, which was unusual, for he rarely gave us things to read.

"You can't make someone read, you. have to discover it for yourself," he wrote inside it. "But if you don't read this and everything else, I'll thrash you. Love, Dad."

I have been chasing my shadow for so long it is only now that I feel it slip within me, like a letter folding into an envelope, a letter I might have written to myself, perhaps, for copyright reasons. Or a deposition, like the one I had to write in Mexico once, after a fight.

What did Marcello tell me? *"La tua vita e un romanzo."* Only he could say something so simple and obvious without making it sound like a cliché. If anyone else had said it, I would have dismissed the notion, or said that my life was less a fiction than a catalogue of events of varying importance, rearranged in order to make it seem less arbitrary. But with Marcello, it's different, somehow. He has a way of saying simple things and meaning them. When he read Dad's *Collects* he told him he should stop writing as he had said all he needed to say.

"Think you missed the point, Marcello," said Dad. But had he?

I can see Marcello now, shuffling along the corridor at the Alabama in his dressing gown and velvet hat. Well, I smiled when he told me my life was a novel. Told him he was probably right.

5

Through the window, raindrops are caught and spread themselves horizontally, flying south at maximum speed, in lines, like the dead heartbeat of an army.

Within the barrage, a sign appears, LA VILLE QUI BOUGE, stuck in a field beside a hedgerow. So. We are not moving at all. It *is* an illusion. In under three hours, LA VILLE QUI BOUGE will have become the only authentic Picardian town in the Beaujolais region and we will still be sitting here, we will sit here for ever, our cigarettes will run out so that no one will be able to tell whether or not we are actually alive; we are stuck, left behind by the moving town, and not even the combined rescue services of Europe, the Euroservices, will be able to save us from complete stasis. Everything is moving, except us. France is moving south, England is moving to Long Island, America is moving in all directions but mostly westwards and the world is moving to one side to avoid any number of collisions, the spinning rocks and debris of history and timelessness hurled at it from all corners of the universe. We are all moving, we are all destroying ourselves, in one way or another, it is our heritage, and who can blame us for it, save God, calling the shots from a safe distance, up above?

Comfort and stability. I have arranged things as best I can with those twin goals in mind. Paper and pencil on the unfolded table. Walkman to the right. Sunglasses and Lucky Light to the left. Can of beer (1664) and reserve miniatures (Martell) above them. Two books, Papini's *Gog* and Yeats' *Collected*, beside the Walkman. Moscontin, Lexomil, Mopral and other palliatives all out of sight, but not out of reach, in the left pocket, to be taken in any order necessary, once or thrice a day, depending on the subject's pain and intuition. And eight "Ramses" condoms in the top pocket, in case eight occasions arise between here and where we – all of us – are headed. There is also, for the record, an uncut *babosa* cactus at my feet, to be magically mixed and augmented some time later, at the other half's.

Is there a doctor on board?

And the compact discs, only one of which I ever listen to – "Spinning Away" being the only track – the four other CDs still awaiting use in their cellophane packing, like the condoms I know I will never use, damn their fingers and thumbs.

I am settling in now. I am achieving a form of equilibrium that comes from a number of factors, the chemicals which flow through my body happily colliding with the natural adrenalin and euphoria produced from travel at maximum speed, from escape and from the crystallization of the past through memory control, acute nostalgia and aesthetic wholeness.

1664.

Lucky Light.

LA VILLE QUI BOUGE.

Maximum Speed.

Field.

Horizontal Raindrops.

1664.

"Spinning Away".

London.

Field.

Flyte.

Field.

Elska.

This is a True Linear Composition of Solitude Management in B Plus Minor, self-addressed letter, hymn to the lost spirits, sub-plot to a story which will attempt to describe the elusive, glacial beauty of Elska, the chicanery of Flyte, the sudden, southern transposition of a northern French town, the advantages and disadvantages of maximum speed, along with a number of other, sundry incidents which, when summarily codified, will serve as a Life of Twist, Irishman, of no current abode. A first novel.

Is there a doctor on board this train?

Through the opposite window, I catch sight of a First World War cemetery, an impossibly sad and neat arrangement, virginal order, crosses over the bones of men half our age fallen in battle, blown up like Myles, or gassed and shot, row upon row of life cut short, dead, collected, buried and lost to the soil. LA VILLE QUI BOUGE now overtakes the cemetery, I can see it in all its maddening detail, its butchers and bakers and candlestick makers all ready and prepared for action, not a hair out of place as they fly past. I smile at them, they cannot see me, they are the ghosts of the future and all the dead soldiers below feel their passing, a waft of hair, occasional flakes of pastry falling as poppies on their heads.

6

I see a single window, I see a thousand windows, all reflecting the same face. A hay bale strikes me a blow to the temple, a train doubles our speed as it rushes back to Paris, while motor cars, even the fastest, fall back as we run parallel to the *autoroute*.

Comfort and stability.

A glance from a stranger seated ahead of me acknowledges my comfort and stability. It is designed to unsettle me; there is a tinge of jealousy, perhaps. Why? Because I took the middle section of the carriage upon entering the train, paying no heed to the seat number printed on my ticket. I have two empty seats in front of me and I have both tables unfolded so that my *effetti essenziali* are spread the way I want them to be. This is the best seat on the train and I feel good in it. Here I can write easily. But not too easily.

Time glides now, it does not pass, it is pushed forwards by travel at maximum speed and by all the lost spirits flying through the air, the moving village, the dead soldiers, the escapers, the forlorn, the damned, the blessed, Flyte in his study, Elska in my arms, all of us lost and then rescued from oblivion by the simple, linear motion of the train.

Flyte turns to me. I hear his deep, deliberate voice from six months ago: "Elska says that love is primarily a projection of need, that I could love anyone and it wouldn't make any difference. She is right, of course. But that's not the point, is it? We go from one person to the next, we know we're falling in love, we know what love is, even if it is a projection of ourselves. But then, some day, someone appears, some spirit, and changes everything. Perhaps it isn't love, perhaps it is infatuation, or something even more dangerous: an obsession. But what does it matter what you call it? It's just words, isn't it?"

Or was it me? Was she talking to me? The memory fades and I know I could be inventing the scene. I am trying to remember exactly how it was, the words are the same but I can't recall whether this is what Elska said, or, rather, whether she said it to me or to Flyte. Perhaps she said it to both of us. What difference does it make, if everything and everyone repeats their actions and words, regardless of whom they are with, if they just go on, blindly, along a track laid out for them?

If it was Flyte talking, remembering what Elska had said to him, does it not provide further evidence of his manipulative nature, of his passion for control? He lacked, he lacks, a number of qualities, but a sense of irony is not one of them. Perhaps, like Elska yesterday, he sought merely to justify himself. Such a desire is foreign to me. "Never regret. Never apologise," I once heard Dad tell Holy God, after the latter had felled a man smaller than himself. "Besides, you're the biggest man in all Ireland. And there's not much you can do about that now, is there?"

Love. Speed. Time. All illusory. I look at my watch, the old Omega Elska gave me which no longer works but which I wear, like a talisman, tightly upon my wrist. The enamel paint has begun to peel from the edge of the watch face and a fragment near the date window has caught the second hand and trapped it. I have no idea when this happened; weeks, months ago. I never had the watch repaired for fear of upsetting the disorder.

I remember now. It was Flyte, not me. Had he suspected

something? Was that why he spoke to me of Elska, of love and infatuation? Was it a message of some sort? Was he trying to corner me?

I move back, further, to two days after the party. I was still settling in. I bought some books. I sat in the Café de Flore, or in my room, reading; I looked up to Montmartre from my balcony, or listened to Marcello in the corridor tell me of the times Dad used to stay at the Alabama when the mammy had had enough of his drinking and ranting, for the old man would often go berserk if the writing happened to fail him or didn't happen at all.

"He would sit in Room 7. And when Bakir cleaned it up after he had left it, he would find scraps of paper under the bed filled with different languages, French, Italian and Irish. I have them all pasted in a book in my room. I'll show it to you one day. When you're ready. It contains a number of interesting *ambulazioni*."

But I couldn't stop thinking of Elska, of her fringe dipped in molten emeralds, and of her smile, as I lay on my bed, imagining. Then Flyte called me.

"So. You were away a long time," he said, briskly.

"A year."

"How was it?"

"New York. It was New York. You know. A lot of late nights. A lot of everything. America. I went out to the Island and looked for tuna. And I stayed."

"I don't like New York."

"Maybe New York doesn't like you."

"So, did you get one?"

"One what?"

"Tuna."

"Next year."

"What are you doing? What are your plans?"

"Nothing in particular. And you? Writing?"

"A little."

"You should do more. You're good at it."

"I ran into Moraes. He's crazy."

"Is he?"

"Sure, he's like you, Twist. Nice crazy, though. You can have either."

"I'll tell him that."

"We're having dinner tomorrow. You're invited."

"Then I'll come."

Part Two

RIP

Part Two

7

Today is the past, then. The Omega proves the fact. And every minute, every second that has marked it, points to an act, an accident which, when brought together on the paper in front of me, will result in a story of infinite order, a seamless reflection of chaos leading up to this journey of maximum speed, this escape to the future, no less uncertain, no less haphazard for being planned in advance.

The only true certainty is the appearance of the other half as he enters Swallows' and is greeted by Sandra. He walks up to the bar and orders a tankard of Guinness. The barman says they no longer possess tankards but Sandra corrects him, disappearing into the kitchen to find one of two she has secreted in a cupboard.

"The boys have to have their Guinness in tankards. Especially today."

I look down at the watch and tap it gently. To my astonishment, the fragment of enamel suddenly falls, allowing the second hand to turn once again. There is nothing to impede its progress now, and I stare at it in wonderment, like a child, as it completes a revolution. I look out through the window, I see a small cloud hanging over the horizon, I look down at my watch again and I see that the cloud is moving, its edgeless outline covering the watch face like a blessing.

I am working my way forwards from that day in July when I saw Elska at the party to eclipse four seasons, picking it all up in the now direction and condensing it into the time it will take me to reach my destination. Why? Because this is the moment, the only moment, the only time to do this. Afterwards, I could be dead or alive. It has to be done now. The future will ultimately lead to a tuna with eyes the size of car headlamps, but I can't think of that now, otherwise I'll be distracted. Mad Joe will have to wait. And so will I.

The story begins at a party and will end at another, exactly one year later. This part of it is Real Time, which is Narrative/ Linear Time conducted at maximum speed, with drinks. This time marks my love affair with Elska and it has a habit of stopping and starting. Control over it is contingent upon life arresting its momentum so that I can get it down on paper. Given that I'm writing into the future, I cannot necessarily promise anything, but as the mammy used to say, "Anyone who can boil an egg without a timer is more than halfway home."

Omega/Enamel Time covers the rest, meaning love and loss and friendship and Paris, which is the perfect place to shed and dry tears, as Joyce and many others knew. Control of it is quite out of the question, but the fixed orbit, Paris, keeps it all going. It's not complicated. But it's not too simple, either, for nothing should ever be too simple, otherwise no one will understand it.

I am leaving, I have left, I am on the road. I have neither home nor love nor money and I still have more of everything than I could ever possibly need. I have the single window, the Walkman, the cigarettes, the medication and the condoms I will never use. I have the memory of Elska. And I have this, my fortieth birthday, which is the future, the past and the present served up for me on a table.

We are now ready to order.

8

Flyte's apartment on rue Jacob was larger than I remembered it. I had been there once before, some years earlier. He had invited me there for a drink after a dinner party to show me some first editions, including an early one of Dad's, *Smārgana-Grānamas*, which I had never seen before. Smythe, the biographer, saw fit to include one of the poems, without permission, in an appendix:

"*A Ragman's Sky
A Patch of Night,
Smārgana-Grānamas
Sewn with Light.*"

It was a nice apartment: from his study you could see the spire of St-Germain-des-Prés and he had a decent collection of art too. Everything was *picobello,* the whisky came in a Waterford crystal tumbler, the cigarettes appeared, as if by magic, from a silver box on the polished coffee table you could see your face in if you wanted; there was not a glossy magazine in sight, everything was how it was supposed to be, sophisticated, old world/new world. Only the Yanks know how to do that, because, strangely, they're the biggest snobs of all. Even more than the bloody English.

Yes, Flyte was American. A few years younger than me, he had the airs and graces of a grandfather. At one time, before

I met him, he had married a Frenchwoman, most probably for convenience, by which I mean he may well have loved the girl but only actually married her in order to do the Paris thing. To a certain extent, all marriages are marriages of convenience, the inconvenience being something one strives to keep locked away somewhere, like the barman and the tankard.

Despite the liaison, I always thought of Flyte as a loner. It was strange to think of him sharing himself with someone, his persona, his belongings, all shipped over the pond so carefully. He seemed to carry his solitude with him, as many American men do. In the Twenties they came over to escape Prohibition, now they come over to escape their women. He was a man of composure and organisation, a bachelor in spirit and habit; there wasn't a chipped plate or a speck of dust to be seen anywhere, and his heart seemed sealed, as if he had suffered some great loss. I was never exactly sure whether I liked him or not, or, indeed, what he might have thought of me, other than the fact that I might have been someone he was expected to get to know, who had a famous father and knew a lot of people.

This may be the future talking, for we actually got on well. I suppose the real reason we were drawn to each other was simple curiosity. In any event, we became friends. He was pretty smooth, a bit of an operator, sharp as a pin, smart, amusing. This was the act. And this is what must have attracted Elska.

He corresponded for magazines in New York on art and other matters. The man was connected. He also wrote fiction occasionally. I once read one of his short stories. It was a love story about a girl's infatuation for a blind man. "A love without vanity," is the line I remember. "What could be more contradictory for a man, more pure for a woman?" What, indeed?

He was less a sentimentalist, if there is such a thing, such a word, than an *amateur* of human emotions, which he was capable of dissecting and arranging with great confidence. All

Americans are confident, it is their birthright, I think it has something to do with their instinct for survival. It is also their tragedy, for in perceiving truth in all they do, they miss the true joy of life, which lies not in certainty, but in mystery. Pragmatists are always short-changed (I am thinking also of Dad's weakness), for there are inevitably fewer answers than questions. I am not sure, now, whether Flyte was actually a pragmatist, since in fact, he did have, does have, something of a poetic spirit; well hidden, of course. It was his humour that brought it out. Wistful, very dry. Perhaps that was it. Elska liked her humour dry.

"You're too serious, Flyte," I must have said to him, once, to wind him up.

"Life is a joke. I suppose that's pretty serious," was his answer. Not bad, I thought, even if he must have said it a dozen times before.

When I arrived at Flyte's, there were three other guests standing in the living room, an attractive blonde, a dark-haired girl and an obvious sort of Frenchman, trying to look interesting, dressed in black, unshaven. They didn't seem to know each other; the blonde was staring at Flyte's bronze elephants on the mantelpiece, the Frenchman was seated, in silence, in an armchair, and the dark-haired girl tried to relax on the sofa, smoking a cigarette as if it were her last.

Flyte led me into the room from the front door. He seemed very relaxed and amused, he was obviously quite pleased with the set-up, a dinner mostly for strangers, calculated to produce an atmosphere to his liking. When he told me Agostini was invited, I was quite surprised. Then it seemed to make sense: he and Elska were old friends, it would provide some stability to the proceedings. Well, I'm sure that was the idea. I know Agostini better than anyone, we've been through things together, and "stable" is not the first word I would use to describe him, certainly not by the end of an evening.

I was right about the man in black. Jean-Pierre. The blonde, Kajfa, was Dutch, the dark-haired girl Spanish, with a name I forget. I was introduced. Elska was in the kitchen, apparently. I took my drink and chatted to Kajfa about the elephants. She thought they were great, she said. She had radiant, smiling eyes. I liked her.

"I don't quite trust them," I said. "I think they're memorising everything."

The fact is, I never really understood where Elska was from, even if I learned her father was Dutch and her mother Finnish. She had been brought up in various unlikely places and had spent hardly any time at all in either Holland or Finland, as her father had been a diplomat. For some reason, I always thought of her as simply Finnish, but that's probably because I got so carried away with the whole Metsalämpi idea; not that I have anything against Rembrandt country, of course. Her father was, in fact, a half, or a quarter, Indonesian, which may go some way to explain my confusion as far as her genes were concerned; maybe there was a hint of Batavia in that faraway gaze of hers. Or is that just me getting carried away again? She was an only child; I couldn't have imagined anything else. As for Kajfa, I assumed she was Elska's friend and that the Frenchman, Jean-Pierre, was Flyte's. As things transpired, of course, he was principally a friend of Elska.

Agostini arrived, waving his arms around as though he'd lost something. I stood with him and Kajfa by the mantelpiece. Kajfa seemed amused by him and started asking him questions while the others listened, keeping their dignity intact.

"Me? I don't do anything really."

"That's nonsense, Agostini," I said. "He takes pictures of pretty girls."

"Well, that's not much, is it?"

"Tell her about the edges, Agostini," I added.

"What are the edges?" asked Kajfa.

"The edges? Nothing, really."

"Tell her, Agostini!"

"The whole thing doesn't mean much. It makes me money. I like the girls, too. Great. But, you know, fashion. It's not exactly interesting, is it?"

Agostini was in a strange mood. The Frenchman was not impressed. The Spanish girl didn't get it either. And Kajfa and me were laughing.

"I'll tell them, Agostini. About the edges. The edges are the most important part. Got to have good edges. Otherwise the pictures are no good."

"That's right, Twist. Who told you that? That's what I said."

"You told me. The other day. I'd hardly put my bag down before you'd explained it to me. But you also explained it to me before I left for America."

Agostini finally relaxed and started laughing too. "I've lost something, somewhere," he said, abstractedly, after a moment.

"You'll find it, Agostini," I said. "Unless it was a girl. You haven't got your heart broken again, have you?"

"I'm not talking about it."

"Was she beautiful?"

"Of course she was beautiful. Too beautiful."

"Beautiful women are always too beautiful. Why don't you go out with someone who's ugly? Be a nice change for you."

Agostini looked around the room. "I need a drink. Where's Flyte?" Then he went off down the hall.

"Do you two always talk to each other like that?" asked Kajfa.

"Like what?"

9

I was left in the room with Kajfa and the two other guests. The Frenchman had begun talking to the Spanish girl. The latter did not speak French, but she confessed to a knowledge of English. The man had a strong accent and the Spanish girl had to lean forward, wrinkling her brow as she did so, in order to understand him. She had a certain beauty to her, a dark beauty, as if she had once committed some terrible crime.

He was a film director: he had made a short film, which had won a prize somewhere, and he was soon to make a longer one. The Spanish girl didn't seem particularly impressed, possibly because she didn't understand what he was saying. He thought he'd played a good hand and he didn't have any cards left. So he tried Kajfa. Soon enough, he was describing Amsterdam to her, another mistake, evidently, as Kajfa knew about Amsterdam already, having been born there. She was kind, though.

"I never thought of it as the Venice of the north. But you might have a point," she said.

Agostini had returned with a drink in his hand. "Venice north? Where's that?"

"Amsterdam," I said.

"Amsterdam?"

Elska now entered the room. I stared at her in disbelief,

for she looked exactly as she had done at the party. She disabled me completely. She glanced at me and then turned to the Frenchman, who had got up from his chair to greet her. They said hello and kissed each other on the cheek. Then she walked over to me and Agostini.

"Hello, Twist. Hello, Agostini. You've met Jean-Pierre, presumably. He just won a prize at a film festival."

I knew Elska was sending him up. It was so obvious to me. I could see through her. Agostini couldn't.

"I don't believe in prizes," he said, emphatically.

Elska came over to us and I put my arm around her and kissed her on the cheek in as relaxed a manner as possible, but I found myself trembling. She had the sweetest scent to her. I looked into her eyes for a moment.

"And you, Elska? Do you believe in prizes?" I could see the Frenchman and the Spanish girl looking over to us.

"But of course! What would the world be without prizes?"

Flyte now appeared, carrying a large plate of melon and cooked ham, which he put on the oval table in an alcove at the end of the room. Then he went off again and returned with a decanter of port. We were seated. I was placed at a diagonal from Elska, between the Spanish girl and the Frenchman.

The dinner followed a path laid out for it by the geometry of contrasting personalities and it soon became clear that Flyte had miscalculated, unless he had actually planned on some kind of confrontation. He certainly hadn't imagined that Agostini possessed such a fighting spirit. The conversation was fragmented and almost arbitrary and I was left with the impression I always have of such occasions, that they are inherently ridiculous. I was there for one reason and one reason alone, which only made it more so. For most of the time, the Frenchman continued talking, dominating the table. He didn't like Hollywood for some reason, but when Agostini asked him what Hollywood was, he didn't seem to have an answer. In fact, no one did, or seemed to care. The Frenchman thought that America unfairly dominated French cinema and didn't necessarily accept Agostini's view that most French directors of the Fifties and Sixties couldn't have got enough of the place. Flyte defended the Frenchman, of course, partly because he was, or could be, a gentleman, and partly because he loved to criticize America, as it indicated a great deal of sophistication on his part. Agostini countered because he was Neapolitan and his occasional need for confrontation was always superior to any views he might have had regarding an argument. "But America invented the Twentieth Century!" he barked.

The Frenchman shouted back – *"C'est ridicule!"* – but to his consternation, Kajfa started laughing uncontrollably, while the Spanish girl looked on, doubtless still wondering how Amsterdam and Venice might be in any way connected to one another, except by water. It was rather like watching a rehearsal for a prize-winning short film. I actually caught the Frenchman making notes on a serviette on his lap at one point, which made the proceedings no less bizarre.

As for me, I watched. All I wanted was to be alone with Elska and I tried not to stare at her too much, listening to the conversation and smiling occasionally.

"What do you think, Twist?" asked the Frenchman.

"About what?"

"About Hollywood?"

"I never go to the cinema, so it's hard for me to say. I prefer the circus."

"You never go to the cinema?"

"Is that so startling?"

Kajfa was still laughing. Perhaps she had smoked a joint earlier. The Frenchman became even more annoyed as it occurred to him that I might have succeeded in impressing the women where he had failed. It was clear I hadn't. Nor had I wished to. Except Elska, of course. This made me his enemy. What he had not understood was that it was going to take a great deal to make an impression, more than he was offering, at least. When the main course was over, I saw my chance and followed Elska into the kitchen on the pretext of helping her.

"Great dinner, Elska."

"You're lying."

"So are you."

"What do you mean?"

"About prizes. Surely you don't believe in prizes?"

"Sometimes."

"Nonsense."

She was smiling. She turned away and took a plate from a cupboard and then faced me. This was the moment, the one that comes back to me as clearly as if it were happening now, as another cemetery appears in the window, only to be cut off, in a flash, by maximum speed.

In that hovering, humming instant of potentiality, our very auras seemed to meet and the promise of all that was possible, all that was impossible, the sum of all that could have happened, and, of course, did happen, between us, came together as we stood there in the kitchen, the sounds of empty chatter echoing from the dining room along the corridor, a serving plate held between us, as if we had become unwitting models in some iconic portrait entitled "Alone at Last". A fraction of space here or there so resolutely implied a kiss that we remained frozen, the moment of sudden complicity arrested. We had become wholly incapable of action, nervous of either eventuality, of transgression or its denial, and time stopped in order to tease us gently, to nudge us into action, offering up an italicized question mark in the air between us. We stayed our distance. As another polemical outburst arose from the dining table, Elska smiled briefly and the plate slipped from our fingers, shattering onto the tiled floor.

"How do you know I don't like prizes?" she asked, abstractedly.

"Do you always mean the opposite of what you say?"

"Yes."

Flyte had appeared in the kitchen to fetch something. "What happened? My Svensson!"

"Nothing," said Elska. "Sorry about the plate. I'll clear it up. Buy you a new one. It was my fault."

"No," said I. "It was mine."

"Ours," said Elska.

"These things happen," Flyte added, moving over to a cupboard and producing a dustpan and brush.

10

In retrospect, in Enamel Time, it seems so unimportant for us to have shied away from that kiss, yet, as I look out to a beam of sunlight falling on the horizon, now severed by the single window, I find myself longing for it to return, again and again; just the moment, that's all, for, by not kissing, Elska and I created a tension far greater than if our lips had actually touched, a tension which transformed the rest of the evening and set a mood for our affair in which all that was not done, not said, merely implied, carried as much weight as what we actually did. "Noted by absence," as Dad would say when one of the locals tripped into the Rally. Vain, implicit potential!

The fact is our imaginings met in a fantasy which made our romance seem both inevitable and doomed from the start. Naturally enough, it was that inevitability that drove us forwards, the perpetual excitement of transgression turning it all into a desultory and vacant reality, which eventually killed our love, stone dead, just as the plate crashed pathetically to the floor, clumsy metaphor awaiting Flyte's pendant brush, dumb parody of desire fresh from the pages of a tuppenny paperback. Svensson plate! What the hell is a Svensson plate?

Did anyone notice our complicity? I doubt it. To me, it was as clear as a pharmacy cross on a winter's night. Kajfa kept laughing, the Frenchman argued in vain to prove himself, and, as

Agostini became more and more drunk, Elska and I looked on as if we were in a separate room, watching it all from a distance, through binoculars, through the noughts. Flyte, meanwhile, tried as best as he could to arbitrate; heated debate was one thing, but this was getting ugly. Inevitably, Agostini got up from his chair.

"*Vai a fare in culo con i tuoi film del cazzo!*"

The Frenchman then rose from his chair and tried to push him. Flyte interceded and Elska and I, along with Kajfa, burst out laughing.

"Don't pick a fight with Agostini, director," said I, composing myself. "It's true he comes from Naples. He'll kill you. Do you want to get killed just because you don't like Hollywood?"

"Don't make it worse, Twist," Flyte said.

"I'm not. *Je veux juste calmer le jeu.*"

That was too much. Now Flyte started laughing. And, partly because Flyte laughed, and partly because he thought Agostini might truly kill him, the Frenchman began laughing too. It was a pathetic sight, as if the man had never laughed before in his life. Agostini cursed; then he stepped away from the table in disgust and turned up the stereo system. It was Elvis, now or never, and soon enough he had taken the Spanish girl by the hand and was dancing along to it, with a big grin on his face.

The Frenchman and Flyte kept up a conversation in which Elska and Kajfa occasionally participated. It was easy for Elska to pacify the Frenchman, he seemed to crumble before her easy wit and immense charm, to such an extent that he was soon apologizing to Agostini for losing his temper. Agostini shook the man's hand with a smile.

"I don't even remember what the fight was about. You should dance more and talk less. Words are a waste of time, anyway. That's why I take pictures. I would kill you if I had to. It's not my fault. I was brought up that way."

The Frenchman then attempted to dance with Kajfa. I watched him lurching from side to side, waving his arms in the air and I remembered one of an endless series of adolescent parties, a record player on the floor, empty cans of beer, a kiss stolen in the corner of a flat somewhere, all lost to a suburb of memory. I considered attempting a dance with Elska, but I didn't have the courage; I had become self-conscious in her presence, the thought of being so close to her again sent a shiver down my spine. I did dance with Kajfa once the Frenchman had returned to his seat. It was only then, strangely, that I noticed Flyte staring at me inquisitively. I sat down again and found myself chatting with Flyte and the Frenchman, trying my damnedest to be normal, smoking a Havana and drinking port, while the others turned on the wooden floor to old records, losing themselves to the drink and the night.

"You're quiet, Twist. I don't know you like this," Flyte said. "Has America changed you? New York usually turns the most modest individual into a raging extrovert. And you are hardly modest."

"I'm thinking, Flyte. That's all."

"It's good to see you, though. You're a mystery. You slip in and out of people's lives so easily. I often think of you as a chameleon."

"Chameleons don't drink port, but I'll accept the analogy. As long as you don't make me stand on a tartan rug. Why are you so opposed to New York? Is it just because that's where you come from? Or is there another reason?"

"I'm not actually against the place. I might even go back. One day."

It was late. I finished my drink and made my excuses. I was tired. I went back to my room at the Alabama, but I couldn't sleep. I drank whisky and read a book. I thought about Dad. I missed him. I thought about him lying in Room 7, staring out through the window or scribbling on bits of paper, wrestling with his imagination, lamenting some quarrel with the mammy, pouring out his heart, pouring in the wine, trying quietly, desperately, to find the right word, or just a syllable, as the dawn appeared at the foot of his single bed.

11

I saw neither Elska nor Flyte for the next month after that dinner. Flyte didn't call. Had he noticed something? Or had I imagined it, was it simply a question of vanity? Maybe there was nothing to it, nothing at all, no imagined kiss, just a plate with a silly name falling through the air. The Frenchman didn't get hurt, and Elska wasn't attracted to me. Nothing. Just me and a fantasy.

I could tell, or thought I could tell, that Flyte was in love with Elska. He looked at her with a mixture of pride and admiration, treating her almost with deference. Yes, that was Flyte in love, all right. Or so I thought. She was perfect, the cat's pyjamas, she fitted into everything so neatly, it was impossibly good, this beauty seated upon the sofa reading *Le Monde* on a Sunday morning, sun streaming through the open window onto the waxed parquet floor, or lying asleep, sublime, untouchable, within linen sheets, her hair spread behind her as if caught in a burst of sea air. She was a first edition, you couldn't find better, not if you spent a lifetime trying. He could do anything with this girl, frame her, immortalize her, embrace her, but above all, look at her from a distance, preferably in company, her intransigent, bewildering elegance reflected perfectly within the mind's eye, Flyte's mind, a clean space for living, monogrammed, sorted, beyond reproach.

He actually said it to me, later. "I'm so proud of her," which is not such a bad thing to say about someone you love, if you mean it, that is. But Flyte said it as if she were a possession and you can never possess a woman, least of all Elska. This was his love. And, inasmuch as it was his way of loving, then there was no doubt that he was in love with her and could not have parted from her. But what of her? I mustn't cheat, for I am already using what I learned later to pass judgement. It's true that, at the time, I would have said much the same thing, or, at least, part of it, but I wouldn't have been so unequivocal about Flyte's attitude, because it's a hard thing to say about someone that they don't know what love is, even if you don't particularly respect them. It's probably the worst thing you can say, in fact. What do I know about love, anyway?

Of course I assumed they were in love. Why else would they have got married? The smile she offered him over that messy dinner table was clearly one of devotion. Flyte is a good-looking man. Any woman would fall for him. Even Elska.

A few days after the dinner, I met up with Agostini. He was happy to talk about them. He always liked Elska. "Elska is so elusive, even when she is in love. I can understand the attraction, it's normal. But Flyte could never hope to possess her. He's such a solitary person, don't you think?"

"I'm not sure I actually know him. But, perhaps, if he really is solitary, then he has the key to it, to make it work. Some women don't need to be possessed, Agostini. You should know that. The whole idea is ridiculous."

"A man has to possess a woman, Twist. Otherwise, there's no point."

"I don't agree. You come from Naples. It's different there."

"It's not different. *È primordiale.*"

"It's not *primordiale*. It's *neanderthale,* for God's sake!"

I didn't want Agostini to know of my infatuation with

Elska. I had told Moraes – well, he'd guessed it – but Moraes was different. I thought if I didn't talk about it, it would be easier to brush it aside, like a dream you can never quite remember but which always stays with you if you decide to make a note of it. And I never write things down. Well, I never used to. Until I got onto this train.

I was settling back into life in Paris. I was supposed to be Flyte's friend. Was it not better to keep Elska as a fantasy, anyway? I could always find a girl if I needed, get Agostini to organize a double date with a couple of noodles; they'd have names like Eva and Natasha, just in from Siberia modelling tights for the Conforama catalogue and they'd be as sweet as pie to us because Agostini would promise them the moon and enthrall them with his edges. No. I wasn't really up for that. Was I?

Why make life complicated? I was free. I had money. I was in Room 76 at the Alabama. Life was easy and July passed in a warm haze as Parisians began to make their way out of town, on their way south. I did nothing of any consequence. I sat in cafés, walked the streets, read books, listened to Marcello, got drunk with Agostini. Thought about the tuna.

Thought about Elska.

I wondered at times why I had come back to Paris, but I knew I was in the right place when I sat, late at night, in reception, listening to Wolf or Régis tell stories, or when I walked the streets at dawn watching the city come to life before my eyes, the clatter of empty refuse bins dumped on the pavement, a waiter rubbing his eyes, a man in an overcoat bringing a glass of beer to shaking lips. My old home. I knew I could be nowhere else, that I was in the right place, one in which I could safely orientate myself, blindfolded if necessary, whatever happened. The tuna could wait.

Some people were saying that Paris wasn't any good anymore.

That it wasn't as good as it used to be, that there was less happening. I never understood this. As much was happening as would ever need to happen. Paris never changes, it is peopled not by transients, by interlopers, but by those who operate it, the barmen, the *garçons*, the shopkeepers, the street sweepers, it is they who ensure it stays alive, it is their job and even a cop will bend the rules the right way to keep it as it should be kept; if the cop is a woman, she may be ugly but seem quite cute and will let you off for throwing someone into a window, or for falling backwards into an art nouveau mirror, if you manage to charm her enough. These are the people I speak to and they speak to me, they give me a drink if I'm broke, they make me laugh when I see death hovering on a corner and they describe to me, through their understanding of this great city, what it is to be alive within its walls. Paris! The only place in the world where I don't have to reinvent myself. Dad was right.

"Agostini! They're saying Paris isn't any good anymore! Imagine!"

"That's for people with nothing better to think about. For people who read magazines."

"You work for magazines!"

"So what? Doesn't mean I have to read them. I'm just doing it for the money."

"You don't need the money. You give most of it away to struggling poets and artists, like that Englishman on Rocket Street."

"That's right. I'm Mother Agostini. But I like the girls and they cost me. One day, I'll marry one of them. I'll take her to Naples and teach her how to cook *al forno*."

12

I take a swig of beer and light another cigarette. I must be careful. Am I getting it right? Is it coming too easily? Mustn't be too easy. Mustn't be too complicated.

A young woman takes the seat opposite. She is blonde and she is wearing too much make-up, yet her eyes are the palest, most translucent green I have ever come across. She takes a cigarette from a packet and places it between her lips. She asks me for a light. I give her one. She smokes her cigarette as if she has been denied the pleasure for a while and she looks through the single window, my single window, as France travels at maximum speed. She appears to avoid me, pretending I do not exist and, as she does so, I look at her for a moment, her face in profile, recalling a girl I once met behind the bar of the Colimore Hotel, Dalkey, when we were eighteen and Dad took us over for a writer's party. "Don't do anything too ostentatious," she said to me, when I had walked her home.

The smoke rises from the young woman's mouth in parallel lines of blueness, reflected in the window. She could only be French but I can't, for the life of me, explain why. Is it her self-assurance? Suddenly, I catch her eye. She finishes her cigarette, gets up and disappears. And I begin writing again.

A couple of weeks passed. After the dinner. Then, one day, I ran into the film director in the rue du Buci. As soon as I saw him, I was caught, by association, within the trap that was my infatuation with Elska. Seeing him brought me closer to her and I entered into conversation with him for no other reason.

"That was quite a dinner, Jacques."

"Jean-Pierre."

"Made your movie yet? Or still collecting prizes for the last one?"

"I'm raising the necessary finance."

"An unenviable task. When you've got the money, why not spend it on something useful?"

"Like a circus?"

"Or a girl."

"I don't need to pay for my women."

"Still got to take them out now and then. Give them a good time."

"So, what do you do?"

"Me? I don't do anything."

"I don't believe you."

"That doesn't change anything. I'll do something at some point. In fact, one day I'm going to go out with Mad Joe and catch a tuna fish with eyes the size of car headlamps."

"Who's Mad Joe?"

"A friend. But you wouldn't like him."

"Why's that?"

"He's American."

"Flyte's American."

"Yeah, but Flyte doesn't like America, does he?"

I bought him a drink at the bar, telling myself I felt sorry for him, for his earnestness and for his lack of humour when, of course, I still clung to the notion that through him I would encounter Elska.

"Why are you buying me a drink if you don't like me?" he asked, holding his glass quite still for a moment.

"I don't know," I said, with a smile. "You're a friend of Flyte? Or of Elska?"

"Both, really."

"You seemed closer to Flyte."

"Flyte was a gentleman that evening. He defended me against that psychopath."

"Agostini's not a psychopath. He's a fashion photographer. How do you know Elska? Just through Flyte?"

"She played a part in a short film I did."

"I didn't know she was an actress."

"She's not. She's a natural."

"A natural? What does that mean?"

"Well, she just acted herself. That's what I wanted."

"What was the part? Is she going to be in any other of your films?"

"She played the lead. A woman who is abandoned by a trickster and takes her revenge."

"How does she do that?"

"She disappears."

"Doesn't sound very convincing. Now who'd go and abandon a pretty girl like that?"

"It's possible."

"Well? Who played the man in it?"

"I did."

"You did? You've got be kidding! I'd like to see that. So, where's it playing?"

"You told me you don't go to the cinema."

"I was joking."

"That wasn't a joke."

"Just tell me where I can see the film."

"I don't have any copies at the moment. But they're going to be showing it soon at the Cinematone on rue des Écoles."

"Does it have a title?"

"Yes, of course. 'La Dernière Goutte'."

"Sounds great. Really."

He seemed pleased at that and bought me a drink. Then I walked back to the Alabama. I couldn't believe it. The man had cast himself as Elska's lover! I had to see this film! Everything and everyone was pointing to her. As I walked through reception, I wasn't in the least surprised to learn that there was a message for me. Flyte had called and asked me to call him back.

13

I called Flyte that evening. He was writing an article about an artist I knew from New York. The artist was called Braine and he had a show up in town, over in the Marais. We arranged to meet for a drink after dinner so I could help him with his article. I suggested a bar. He insisted I come to his house. I got to the apartment at midnight. He poured me a drink and we sat in his study. He had a huge desk with neat piles of papers and books on it.

"Where's Elska?"

"She went out to dinner."

"I didn't know she was an actress."

"She's not. She just acted once, in Jean-Pierre's film."

"Any good?"

"Elska enjoyed doing it, that was the point. These short films almost always fail, even when they win prizes. They always have to have an ending."

"They're not going to be very short without one, are they?"

"You know what I mean. A *dénouement*. I wasn't too happy about Elska doing it. It was just after we'd met. She thought I was being possessive."

"You weren't?"

"Of course not. I'm not like that. I just thought it was below her. But then, I can't tell her anything. I learned that. I mean, why should I?"

"What's he like, Jean-Pierre?"

"You met him."

"Yes, of course. And I ran into him again. But I didn't get the measure of him. I mean, he cast himself in his own film. What do you make of that?"

"Perhaps he was on a budget?" Flyte laughed.

Flyte's laugh was infectious, you couldn't help but join in. He was the consummate host, even when I was the only guest. He was always acting the part. He was a sport, that's what he was. A sport. He belonged to another age. It was true, he looked just like his grandfather, the publisher, whose photograph was in a large, silver frame on a shelf behind him. They were practically twins to look at, one in black and white, one in colour. He was, of course, aloof, abstracted from his emotions, as his grandfather appeared, but there was more to it than that, more than a simple repetition of airs and graces through upbringing; everything about him was old, his pretensions as a writer, modest, unassuming, his acceptance of himself as an amateur in a world so crowded with opportunism and self-aggrandisement. In this he was perhaps less of an actor; the strange thing was that although he didn't think of himself as a writer, a real writer, he actually was; his stories have a delightful, elliptical touch to them, an understatement and subtlety that sets them apart from the colloquial typewriting of his peers.

He sat at his desk, smoking and drinking from a crystal tumbler of bourbon and, in the half-light of the room, I could be forgiven for thinking I really was in another age, one in which manners clothed desire and words disguised meaning. He and I had always acted out our encounters, never more so than on that evening.

"And you, Twist?"

"Me?"

"What happened to you lately?"

"Nothing. I just keep moving. I have to."

"Why?"

"I don't know. Chasing my shadow, maybe."

"That can be tiring."

"I can take it."

"Sure."

"So, what about this film, then? With Elska?"

"She won't let me see it."

"But I bet you have."

Flyte smiled. He took a swig of bourbon and turned to a sheaf of papers on his desk. "What about Braine?"

"Braine's an upright. He keeps on saying, 'Why don't people paint anymore? What's wrong with painting all of a sudden?' He sees history as ineluctable, not something you can avoid if it doesn't happen to suit your purposes. For example, he says you can't be an artist and not spend some time looking at Rembrandt. You can't say it's old-fashioned or something. But then, art has been hijacked by fashion and soon all Rembrandt will be remembered for is his hats, anyway. You can buy anything these days, so why not art? As for Braine, he accepts repetition and has no interest in originality. I can't believe they've given him a show. Don't tell me he's going to become fashionable? Still, at least it'll help him pay for the bills and the benders. Why are you still writing about art, anyway? You should just write stories. You're good at it. And you don't need the money. Not with grandpa behind you."

"What? You don't think I'm any good at it?"

"Don't be so defensive. You know that's not what I meant."

"Perhaps. Do me a favour, Twist."

"Another? Tell me what it is first."

"It's Elska. She's not communicating with me. Perhaps you could take her out for lunch or something. As my guest, of course."

"Why me?"

"I want to know what she's thinking. We are hardly speaking at the moment. I don't understand what's happened to us."

"Wouldn't it be better if she spoke to a girlfriend? Or something?"

"A girlfriend isn't going to speak to me, is she?"

"What about Kajfa?"

"No. Wouldn't work."

"So, why me? What makes you think she'll talk to me?"

"She likes you."

"Any more favours, Flyte?"

"No. That's it." Flyte laughed, which made the situation somehow easier for me to handle. After all, how was I supposed to react to that? What was I supposed to say? Exactly? That I couldn't have lunch with Elska because I was infatuated with her? Of course, I could have excused myself by saying I couldn't possibly act as Flyte's spy. But Flyte was a friend. And when a friend asks a favour of you, you have to do it. If the favour is impossible, then the friend is not a friend, after all. A classic favour is usually a problem, a dilemma involving divided loyalty. Yet here, placed in my lap, was a favour not even I could have dreamed up.

"What is it, Flyte?" I said, stalling. "You think she's having an affair?"

"No."

"Be honest."

"No, it's not that."

"Good. Because women only discuss affairs with their nearest girlfriend. And I'm a long way down the hierarchy."

"I just want to know what she's thinking."

"Of you?"

"Not just me."

"You're not being honest with me, Flyte."

"I am. It's simple. Why can't you accept that?"

"There's nothing simple about relationships between men and women. You can't pretend to be naive all of a sudden."

"So, you can't do it."

"Of course I'll do it."

"Thanks. We're going away in August. But we're not leaving for a week. Why not call her tomorrow? You can say it's about work."

"Work?"

"Films. Acting."

"I don't act anymore. I stopped ages ago."

"Well, perhaps you can come out of retirement for the duration of a lunch. Make something up."

It was late. Elska still hadn't returned. I didn't want to be there when she did. Perhaps she *was* having an affair. No. People don't have affairs at night. Affairs are conducted during the afternoon. *Cinq à sept.* What did Flyte really want to know? Was he calling my bluff? Was that it?

I walked back slowly to the Alabama. The bars were closing, but Gérard unlocked the door at the Armistice for me and gave me a glass of Bordeaux.

"You were away. What was it like?"

"I was in New York, Gérard. New York is a great city. But as Lowry said, it favours the short haul."

"Lowry?"

"Yes, Lowry. *Under the Volcano.*"

"Of course."

"Mind you, he's not the best of role models. He ended up in Bellevue, which is a mental hospital. They put Caitlin Thomas in there after Dylan copped it. Then they stuck up a nice plaque for the poet, outside the Chelsea Hotel. They gave Brendan Behan one as well. Behan thought he should get a mention. He said, 'I am not humble enough to say I do not deserve one.'"

"Deserve what?"

"A plaque, Gérard. It's like a medal. For a building. Well, Behan deserved one all right. I think Dad met him and they got drunk together."

"Your father was a great man."

"I know, Gérard. I know."

"Are you still acting, Seamus?"

"No, I stopped. You know, you're the only person who calls me Seamus. Apart from at the Alabama. Everyone else calls me Twist."

"You're too young to retire."

"No one's too young to retire."

"So, what now?"

"I'm going to have an affair. A love affair."

"That should keep you busy."

"I'll see. I've never really had one before. I mean, a proper one."

Part Three
TRIP

14

I walked back to the Alabama confused, intrigued by my drink with Flyte. With hindsight, of course, I can make sense of it. But not then.

I sat in reception with Wolf, listening to his stories, trying to forget all that went on outside the walls of the hotel. The Alabama is my refuge. Once I have been let through that door, I am cut off from the world and caught within a microcosm in which Paris becomes distant, refracted, only perceived through the large window facing the street and the market, or, through the grille of my balcony up above, north to Sacré Coeur or south to the Sénat. When Dad stayed on those fathomless nights, his view was from the first floor; each corner of the Alabama offers a different perspective, but it is all the Alabama's Paris, whichever way you like to look at it.

Wolf was leaning forwards on the reception desk, rolling a cigarette and looking distinctly animated. "I saw a man make love to a woman against the window last night. I don't know who the man was. I thought perhaps I'd seen him somewhere before. I think he's from the neighbourhood. He came past the hotel earlier in the evening and picked up a middle-aged tourist staying in 36 as she left through the front door. Just like that. He must have taken her out for a meal. I saw them later at the market bar; he was plying her with drinks and making her laugh.

Then he walked her up the street to the window and stood with her against the window. They started kissing. Then he lifted up her skirt and made love to her, I mean, he actually nailed her, right there, in front of me. People forget it's a window for some reason, they just don't realize they can be seen. What do you make of that, Seamus? Is it normal for English women to do that?"

"What? Make love?"

"You know what I mean. Right there. In public."

"How do I know? I'm Irish, aren't I?" I thought for a moment. Wolf wanted an answer. "I think it's more of a Paris story. You get arrested for that in England."

"Arrested? For making love? What do they do with you when you rob a bank?"

I went upstairs and sat in my room. I couldn't sleep. I stood on the balcony looking into the sky. It was hot. I felt detached from everything, I could no longer define myself; my return to Paris had begun to have an insidious effect upon me. Too many people all of a sudden. Too many personalities. And I couldn't stop thinking about Dad, lying below, his ghost working through the night, turning it into an elegy of love and loss. *"The Blood is thicker than the Water/Thicker than the Sea..."*

I should have been pleased. After all, I was going to have a love affair with the most beautiful woman I had ever seen. Yet I was full of trepidation. I don't know why. I couldn't pinpoint it then and I certainly can't now, eleven months later, here, within the clinical abstraction of a speeding train. But I do remember feeling, for the first time in my life, insecure, unsure of myself. All those years of acting could never have prepared me for that yawning moment of emptiness. Then I snapped out of it, probably finished my drink and finally, as first light slipped like a burglar through the window, found that simplest, most elusive pleasure. Sleep.

It was late morning when I awoke. I lit a cigarette and called Flyte's apartment.

"I'll just get her for you, Twist."

"Hello," came Elska's voice.

"Want to have lunch? Talk about work?"

"Work?"

"You know. Acting. Films. Prizes. That kind of thing."

"Flyte told me you wanted to see me."

"Well?"

"Sure. When?"

"Today."

"Fine."

I reserved a table at a local brasserie for one-thirty and took a shower. When I put my suit jacket on and searched for a cigarette I found an envelope, with some money in it and a note from Flyte. "Please don't be insulted. But I said I would invite you."

Elska was late. While I sat waiting, I remembered those times, earlier, when I had been with her, a stranger. When did I first meet her? Ten years ago? There was a dinner somewhere. No. It wasn't a dinner. She was on the terrace of a café, alone, and I was walking past with Agostini, who already knew her. We shook hands. But we didn't really talk. We never talked, during the many occasions we found ourselves in the same place. We just smiled at one another. How odd to have become familiar with someone without ever having conversed!

Two or three years later, Elska had an affair with a Spaniard, Ernesto, who was an acquaintance of mine. It didn't last very long, but I had dinner with them several times. I'm not sure how she felt about Ernesto, and Ernesto, being an aristocrat, rarely spoke his heart to me. He did tell me it was she who ended it, however. But I already knew that.

During those dinners, we were invariably joined by others,

so I would spend my time talking to Ernesto, or someone else, rather than Elska. It's strange, I'm remembering through the act of writing, I'd completely ignored Ernesto and Elska earlier. I'm also cheating, of course, because I very much doubted I thought about Ernesto while I waited for Elska to appear. Is this what they call poetic licence? Dad always found that very funny.

I must have talked to Elska at some point. Once, as we were leaving a restaurant after dining with Ernesto and some others, Elska turned to me. That's right. She confided in me: "We keep on seeing each other. But we never talk. Funny."

"Perhaps it's better like that."

"Because there's nothing to talk about?"

"Because we'd probably argue. Then again, perhaps not."

"You're a close friend of Ernesto, aren't you?"

"A friend. Yes."

"I'm leaving him. Don't be angry with me."

"It's nothing to do with me, Elska. I don't have to know. In fact, I don't even know why you're telling me."

She was a little drunk. It wasn't that her speech was slurred, it was the slight uncertainty in her voice and, of course, the fact that she was behaving so out of character, so suddenly becoming intimate with me. It was the only time I ever saw her like that. Ever.

15

So there I was, waiting in the brasserie, watching the clock on the wall and wondering quite what it was Flyte expected of me. The idea of a test took root in my mind. Yes, he was testing me. Or testing her. Or both of us, perhaps. But no, that wasn't like Flyte. He was too sophisticated for such things, wasn't he? Too much of a sport.

Then Elska appeared. And I knew at once I hadn't imagined that moment of shared desire in the kitchen. I stood up for her as the waiter pulled the table out so that she could sit on the *banquette*.

She looked radiant, of course. She was wearing a blue suit and a cream silk shirt tied at the collar and her entire bearing was of such elegance I wondered how any woman could comfortably stand in the same room as her. She had dispensed with her emerald fringe, it was black now, pure black, and her hair fell effortlessly over her shoulders. Her eyes sparkled, her mouth was set in a knowing grin as she took her seat and faced me and her lips were glossed with pale pink lipstick. We kissed on the cheek, almost as an afterthought. She settled onto the *banquette* and sat perfectly still for a moment, staring into my eyes. Then she produced a cigarette from her bag and I lit it for her.

"You're nervous, Twist. I've never seen you nervous before. Twist? Nervous? Impossible!" She smiled again, more broadly.

"We're going to have a love affair. It's decided." She didn't falter. I might have been discussing a news item. "Actually, we've already begun it. The shaking plate scene. Like a drink? *Coupe?*"

"Why not?" she asked, abstractedly.

I ordered. She was still smiling. The drinks came and we clinked glasses. "You're an actress. How about that?"

"I'm not an actress. No."

"But the unshaven director turned you into one."

"The unshaven director asked me to be myself in a film with an ending. That's all."

"The only time people really act is when they are told to play themselves."

"That's too clever by half."

"It's true. They can be more honest; then it all comes out. Is that what you did? Pretend to be you?"

"That's for you to decide. After all, you seem to be making all the decisions around here."

"Cheers, Elska!" I said, taking a sip of champagne. "That was a great dinner we had."

"Cheers!"

"I mean, no one got killed."

"Agostini would never kill anyone. I know him pretty well, you know."

"So do I. Don't be so sure."

"Agostini is wonderful. But he's all talk."

"But Agostini is an upright. He means what he says."

"What's an upright?"

"The world is divided between uprights and everyone else. Agostini's an upright. So's Moraes. And a few others. Braine, for example."

"And you, presumably?"

"That's not for me to say."

"Can women be uprights?"

"I don't know. I've never thought of it. I suppose so. If they can be, then you're an upright. No question about it. I'll have to ask Braine."

"He's in charge, is he?"

"I think he invented it, yes."

"Sounds a little childish."

"Men are childish."

"What about Flyte?"

"Childish?"

"No. Upright?"

"But of course."

"You're just being diplomatic."

The waiter came and we ordered. Elska chose salmon.

"You said you wanted to talk to me about something. Films and prizes. Or did you simply want to provoke me? I wasn't expecting such an interesting lunch. It's funny, we've never really spoken to each other. And I've never actually seen you with a woman."

"It is strange, all that. But stranger things have happened. I'm an identical twin. I suppose that's got something to do with it. With the fact I never married."

"But you must have girlfriends?"

"Occasionally."

"Just girls, then. Like Agostini?"

"That's right. Just girls." Elska laughed.

"Flyte loves you, doesn't he? I mean, very much?"

"Does he? Is this his idea? This lunch of surprises?"

"Of course not."

"You're lying."

"I don't lie. I do a lot of things. But I don't lie. Let's not talk about it. I wanted to see you. And that's the truth."

"I often walk past the Hotel Alabama and wonder if you are there. Is that where you live now?"

"I've always lived there in a sense. My father used to take us when we were children. He would stay there and write sometimes."

"He's very important to you, isn't he?"

"All fathers are important, aren't they? We spend most of our lives trying to meet their expectations even when we don't really understand what those expectations might be."

"So, what did your father expect of you?"

"I don't know. He never told me. He was a contradiction. Full of opposites. Loud and private, loving and selfish, idealistic and destructive. The whole works. But he was a great poet and a great man and I can't get him out of my head. Not his words nor his writing nor his maddening habit of never telling me what he expected of me."

"Is that important? To do what is expected?"

"Possibly. At least so you can do the opposite. I actually wanted to be a lion-tamer when I was young. Tiger-tamer, to be more precise. But I never dared tell anyone. I was afraid they'd laugh at me."

Elska smiled. "I can't imagine you being afraid of being laughed at."

"There's laughter and there's laughter, isn't there? What about your father?"

"A diplomat."

"That's right. I imagine he wanted you to marry well, have children, be looked after."

"Be content, mainly."

"What about Finland? Don't you lot get very sad up there, in the ice and the gloom?"

"I like it. It's not gloomy at all. Clear as crystal as a matter of fact."

"How's your salmon?"

"The salmon was a safe bet. Why aren't you eating?"

"I can't concentrate."

"You're thinking about our affair that hasn't happened?"

"No. I'm thinking about our affair that has already started. What are you doing this afternoon?"

"That's a leading question."

"Well?"

"Nothing. Yet."

"Let's go to the movies."

"You don't go to the movies. You only go to the circus."

Elska laughed, I can see her now, her laughter filtering through the seasons, rushing, now racing, to catch up with me, right through the lead of my Walkman and into my ears, drowning out every note of "Spinning Away" as it does so.

"That's right. Well, let's do something else."

16

We sat in the brasserie, talking well into the afternoon. Then we went into the Gardens. We had drunk a bottle of Bordeaux and had another couple of glasses afterwards as we sat there having a conversation we could have had ten years earlier but didn't.

Elska told me about her life, about her upbringing in different places, in Washington DC, Lisbon, Bangkok. Her childhood was a solitary one, she read and she danced and she was healthy and everything seemed to match the view I had formed of her; there wasn't a surprise in it, only the fact that she had ended up with a sport for a husband, and even that began to make sense somehow, for it revealed a desire for security, which is not a weakness necessarily, even if there was clearly a lack of passion in it. We didn't talk about that. I regretted mentioning Flyte over lunch and made a vow never to mention his name again. Isn't it the first rule with affairs? Never talk about the other side?

As we walked through the Gardens, we made jokes about Paris and the French and the people we knew. We looked down the avenue of trees that led up to the Closerie and we described, together, an imaginary portrait of it all, taken by Agostini, edges included. And, later, I stopped her in her tracks on an impulse and told her she hadn't broken Ernesto's heart, that he was perhaps one of the only men who had got over her.

"You make me out to be a *femme fatale*, which I am not. I ask nothing of men."

"That's asking a lot."

"What do you mean?"

"Men like to give, otherwise they feel useless."

"I don't believe in such things. Rules. Everyone's different, after all."

We sat on a pair of chairs hidden in the shade of a huge oak tree and we watched as people passed, wondering what sort of lives they led. He sells mobile telephones. He works in a bank. No, in a post office. And he is an *intellectuel engagé*, which means he thinks pretty girls are interested in politics.

"And you? What sort of life do you lead, Elska?"

"Simple."

"You let life come to you. Is that the idea?"

"Roughly speaking. I don't have a job, if that's what you mean. People are always shocked by that. Women are supposed to work now; I mean, they have to work. What kind of freedom is that? I don't have to, so I don't. My life was always rather chaotic. I never knew where home was because of being brought up in so many different places. I had no brothers or sisters so I was left to my own devices. My father married my mother late in life; she was his second wife. His first wife died. I don't think he ever got over it."

"But he loved your mother?"

"Of course. But that didn't stop him yearning. My mother told me after he died. She accepted it. That was her genius. It still is. To accept the fact, for it was a fact, and to keep her dignity. I think she always knew it. From the beginning. She understood that you could only really love once in your life, that you could tell yourself you were falling in love again and again, but that you were just searching, trying to rediscover some lost love from the past."

"Do you believe that?"

"That's how it was with my father. I once saw a photograph of his first wife, his true love. It fell out of his wallet when we were at the beach. My mother didn't see it. But I did. He put the photograph back in his wallet and turned away from me. I was twelve, or thirteen, at the time. I didn't think anything of it for some reason. But I remembered it when my mother told me what the truth was. Life is like that, don't you think? Clues thrown up for us. Sometimes we catch them, sometimes we don't. That clue was so obvious, but I would never have accepted it at the time."

"And do you accept it now?"

"Yes, I suppose so. I just find it so poignant, so sad and romantic."

Her eyes had a distant look to them, a sudden frailty. Yes, there was a frailty to Elska somewhere, deeply hidden, beyond her grasp, beyond mine, and, even if it were inexplicable, it still existed; that is all that mattered. No one could possibly be that composed all the time and the proof was in that moment when I first saw in her expression an opening to her heart.

"Do you believe it's true, then?" I persisted.

"What?"

"That you only have one love and that you spend the rest of your life trying to recreate it?"

"I don't know."

"I think you do."

"I might believe it. But I'm not sure whether it ever happened to me."

"My parents loved each other," I said, looking away for a moment and recalling those perpetually sunny days when we would walk, all five of us, through the Gardens together, the mammy leading us onwards, Dad lagging behind, looking up into the sky.

"I don't think my father was ever with another woman. He wasn't really interested in women, particularly. He would often write about them, but it was always one woman, in various guises: my mother, or his idea of her, an illusion he had fostered since the day he met her, when he was a student in Dublin. Even if things were bad and they had fought, he would still write about this imaginary woman, this archetype, and the letters he wrote to my mother when he was away were all part of it, part of this great bubbling, epic fantasy which was his love for her. The mammy died two weeks after he did, broken-hearted. The letters were all the same, I only needed to read one of them, but I went through most of them nonetheless. Marcello, the old Italian actor at the Alabama, told my father he could stop writing at one point because he had said all that was needed to say. Strange to think of art being somehow finite, an entire vocabulary of expression capable of ending, of being encapsulated, within the cloth covers of one thin volume, but it's often like that. So, in a way, Marcello was right, for Dad was simply making a portrait of a woman he loved who happened to be the mammy, a portrait he actually finished long before dying. It was a paradigm, a fiction, but it was still the mammy."

"I read your father's poetry. He talks about the sea."

"The sea was the thing. And that's where I go sometimes. I am trying to get something from it. It could be a tuna with eyes the size of car headlamps. Or it could be something else. Just the idea of it. That may well prove sufficient. Ideas of things often are. Actually, they're often better. Like our kiss."

"Our kiss?"

"In the kitchen."

"We didn't kiss."

"We could have kissed. That's what counts. But there was the problem of the plate, wasn't there? The Svensson plate."

We sat in silence for a while, smoking and looking up

through the tree to the infinite blueness of the August sky. I stubbed out my cigarette on the gravel. I took hers and stubbed it out. And then I kissed her.

17

She could have slapped me. She should have slapped me. But she didn't. She allowed me to kiss her as if it were the most natural thing in the world, as if there were nothing else for us to do.

I put my arm around her shoulder and felt the back of her neck through her thick, black hair, and I felt the inside pink of her mouth, her tongue, the fullness of her and the tenderness and she responded, not in the least surprised by my temerity, rather rushing towards it, so that our kiss became frantic, adolescent almost. Her eyes closed, the Gardens disappeared, I felt her breast, burying my hand under her jacket and we fled into that desire postponed from the dinner, that ridiculous dinner, a month earlier, and all the presumption, all the expectation, met in a coordinated act of abandon seemingly beyond our control.

Desire! It takes on a life of its own, so easily propelling us beyond ourselves into that void of clumsiness and deceit, a no man's land of uncertainty in which friend and foe become indivisible. And, as it does so, our true selves are left behind, or what we like to think of as our true selves, for, if we fear the act itself, we stand in dread of registering that dark, unknown hemisphere of our being, that part of our soul ignored, dormant, which actually propels us forwards, backwards, sideways; we are, with just a kiss, no longer what we thought, we have been subjugated by an impulse, an obsession, an instinct, which transforms us, not into something of complexity, of duality, but into the simplest of beings, just a man, a woman, reaching over the edge for some kind of satiation.

Am I exaggerating? Possibly. But to become what they used to call a cad in the time it took me to move my head an aura's width towards Elska and kiss her like that is to see a world turned upside down, a world which was already spinning away, and to see guilt as surely as if it were a household object lying in pieces on the floor. To brush that guilt aside, see it relinquished through some hopeless justification of the act, is to know that, whatever our ideals, whatever we might think of ourselves, we are all eventually reduced to actors in a short film of the most prize-winning banality. Banal? Of course! For, when we lose control, we often become less, not more, interesting.

This is what I thought then. Not now. Everything is different now. Non-corroborating evidence has altered the picture somewhat. What remains true is that the excitement transgression brings for its own sake is a very different matter to simple desire. Nothing is exact or neatly divisible, but we always endeavour to organize our emotions that way, another deception of course, amongst the Himalayan mountain range of others.

Past and present now hold hands and I feel a muted chuckle of release through my body, here on the train, joining Elska's laughter as a small, dead branch, acting on cue, falls neatly into her lap, causing her to break away and interrupting our kiss. Strange conspiracy! Nature's inadvertent caveat!

Another kiss. Then another, no less wholesome than the others. And silence. I turned to her, got up from the chair and took her arm. We were then obliged to retrace our steps, for the hotel I had in mind was located in rue de Médicis.

18

This train is going too fast. And the faster it goes, the less I feel there is someone in control of it. How can any one person drive this beast? I see the devil himself, reeking of some noxious aftershave, perhaps his own concoction, now available in a horned bottle, lining up another row of pylons for destruction. The sleek, silvery bow buries itself in the greenscape and all hands turn to the *brise-vitres*, shiny, red hammers plucked from their sockets, drinks and gift trolleys dance through the air, miniatures and Euroteddies embarking on a short, desperate waltz before crashing to the upturned ceiling. I adjust my tie and step out into a new world. Could be Eire. Raindrops, laughter, Dad licking his lips, Holy God bending down to me from the bar with a question and a pat of the ham hand.

"No, sir. I haven't decided what to do yet."

I am thinking of that walk to the hotel – not the Alabama, that would have been to advertise our deceit – silent journey of another destruction, construction. Families passed, their motion slowed through memory, knowing faces turned towards us, a boy on roller skates, a tourist stopping to light a cigarette as the two of us walked on, willy-nilly, oblivious.

Elska's skin had a smoothness and tautness to it that made me think of silk, tailored for me and for me alone. I search in vain for the way she felt to me, yet all I can muster is a weak analogy, a groping through the dark which is at once hapless and forlorn. I see her now caressed by another, I stand beside a foreign bed looking down as my successor, my predecessor, rediscovers what I discovered, for at least *that* is an absolute, the body of Elska, whichever way you look at it, in whatever manner you enter it, for one enters a body as one enters a space, it is a shrine of personality and, once entered, can never be truly forgotten. There will always be a moment when a flash of longing might be triggered, the feeling of loss brought into focus so sharp I close my eyes and pray for extinction. It passes, like all things, this torture of hindsight, turning us all into budding masochists, for the torture is always followed by regret:

"Beware the Bite of Sadness
As Sadness bares her Teeth,
Beware the Bite of Sadness
The Part that lies Beneath."

With each landmark, each hill, each pylon miraculously circumvented, each tree, each bale of hay, I time the movements of some monstrous interloper as he pushes himself into Elska, his unwashed paws and eager erection niftily teased by the hand of her whom I once possessed, whose shadowy profile I accompanied to the room at the top of the hotel where, according to the brochure, Verlaine emptied his heart, or his guts, and where, at other times, a million other couples seized the moment, took their desire for a walk and eventually parted company with it, lost it, watched it disappear across the street and into the Gardens. Breakfast not included.

My fumblings with memory are only equalled by those first, desperate fumblings with an erotic transformation of Elska. One should always be careful not to damage clothing or leave traceable marks upon the flesh, a kiss converted through some subconscious rage into a stain of evidence, and my efforts in that department, while by no means compromising my ardour, were appreciated by all parties. Even cads have principles.

Elska's body, now upon the bed, falling through Enamel Time to a position best suited for examination, the post-mortem of desire, comes to me now as I come towards it, seated beside her, now bending to caress its forgiving contours, my hand upon a breast, now upon a thigh, a kiss lost amongst so many others, the teasing of fantasy into fact, true collision of the actual and the transcendental, the increasing leaps of imagination making of me the absolute voyeur of myself, and of all those others whose passion I shared, a line of lovers stretching from me to adolescence, to that very first time when Elska unhooked her gym slip and surrendered, most probably to some earnest and footsome tennis player called Gustav behind the practice wall.

But suddenly, I cannot picture anyone making love to her, imagined or real, not even Flyte; especially Flyte, for some reason. Only me. Is that the greatest illusion, delusion? Who can say?

The real deception was that she offered me herself as if I really were the only one. And I accepted her as such. I lost all that I was as I entered her, I could only think of the present, the gift of timelessness, I drove myself into her with a conviction which defied everything, all thought, all recrimination, and she took me, she received me, gladly, turning for me, kneeling upon that eternally unmade bed, and I grasped her by the hips and looked down at her head, turned to the side, the corner of an eye, or of her mouth, revealing not a trace of what she must have thought, if she thought at all, if, as I suspect, she too found herself lost and drowning in an ocean sea of desire. Even now, in this prison cockpit of over-maximum speed, I feel the same stirring as I recall those tantalising close-ups and reverses, as I watch, undaunted, the B roll of some greater film, never to be exposed, which is my imagination, unexpurgated.

I lay upon my back and she placed her hands upon my shoulders, looking up, looking into my eyes, then looking right through me, as if I had become transparent, as if all my character, my personality, had been flattened as surely as I was flattened on that mattress, a man bereft of all reason thrashing through the torment of his longing. Our bodies sweated, our hands gripped each other, our knuckles showed white, we were caught in a foreign place, by a love which rose in a perspiring cloudlet, hiding us from everyone and everything.

"Where is it? The place? Then?" I asked.

"It's a wood. By a lake."

"Finland?"

"Yes. Finland."

"Is it cold?"

"Not always."

"Does it have a name? Or did you make it up?"

"Everywhere has a name."

"So? What is it?"

"Metsalämpi."

Part Four

RIPE

19

She's come back. The girl. The woman. She must be sitting with a non-smoker. Boyfriend? Husband? She must be with someone. Unless she's one of those people who can't stand being in a smoking section, even though they smoke. Or one of the others who feel they have to stick to their seat number. This I doubt, for I am convinced she is French and not the kind of person to worry about things like seat numbers. No. She's with someone, a man who bought her ticket for her. They met the previous evening somewhere and he invited her to London for a couple of days. He's on business but she can go shopping, get herself a pair of hipsters and a T-shirt with COOL emblazoned upon it.

She puts the cigarette to her lips. Now she's staring right at me. I offer her a light and she takes it. She turns towards the window. My window. And she looks out, through her reflection. She looks good when she does that. Very good. I remove my headphones and place them on the woman's head. Then I turn up the volume a little. I take one of the Martell miniatures and unscrew the top. Then I push it across the table. She shakes her head and draws on her cigarette languidly. She looks through the window again. Then she stubs out her cigarette in the ashtray on the armrest of her seat. She takes off the headphones and gives them back to me with a smile, gets up from her seat and walks back to her compartment. A thin line of smoke still rises from the ashtray. I take the Martell miniature and drink of its contents. Then I put the headphones back on, set the music to the beginning of the song, for the thousandth time, and resume the act of scribbling, switching from Narrative Time to Enamel Time with the first mark of pencil on the paper.

As I do so, it occurs to me that the girl never really sat opposite me, it was an illusion, confirmed by the Memory Mash mechanism on the Walkman. But if I want her to come back, I can summon her up with the Skip and Search button. Life is so much easier than it was before, now that we have the technology. I've even got rechargeable batteries, I'm like Myles was with the toy pistol and no one's taking it off me on pain of death. Except the girl, if she wants. Then I won't have to think of Elska, I can think of something else, perhaps. But wait! She *was* there, opposite me, the smoke is still rising from the ashtray for the express purpose of proving the fact!

"Just enjoy them, Seamus," I can hear Marcello tell me. "Don't get involved. Just admire them. You don't have to fall in love. Look at me. I'm eighty-two. And I can honestly say I have only been in love on one occasion. Strange? Not necessarily."

"It's too late for me now, Marcello. *Troppo tarde!*"

Marcello lived in the Alabama for forty-seven years. Max gave him a room at the back, number 49, and he would lose himself there, when he was not walking the corridors, amidst the memorabilia of a life spent in impersonation. Marcello and Dad were great friends and I always listen to what he has to say. Dad looked up to him. And that was a rare thing for him to do. "Marcello has the gift of the gab. At least half of what he says makes perfect sense." When I get to London, practically the first thing I will do is tell the other half some of the things Marcello said to me. He will want to know. Marcello was always very important to us. And I will give him the scrapbook too, as a present.

London! I may not last long there. London is not such a foreign city, but I am foreign in it. London is swinging but I don't understand what anyone is saying or how it swings, although the other half and I, along with Sandra, may well swing for a moment or two in the restaurant. London is lurching, not swinging. Lurching London. The cabbie will tell me it is too hot, too cold, too wet, everyone will speak in a code designed to camouflage desire, I will walk the streets waiting for something strange, but not necessarily interesting, to happen, the bars will close too early and I will encounter a girl called Bella who will guide me through the night, turning it into a journey, her smile will become a kiss and the dawn will break without either of us even realizing it.

I could always buy an air ticket to Rio and sit in Moraes' garden in a hammock. I will write a song on love and loss as I swing there, looking up through the trees, and perhaps one about a man who wishes to change the world by making a triangular extension to a lake in order to accommodate the reflection of a mountain summit. Then I will send the songs by fax to the man with the ponytail at the Crest Hotel in Sag Harbor. He can choose the one he wants and fax me back comments if he likes, if he finds that a word here or there doesn't quite work with the music he has in mind, for example. Sometimes, you have to be prepared to compromise in business.

Or I will go to New York City and sort it out directly, with the aid of my friendly lawyer, Mr Steinglitz. Then I will ride in a yellow cab up Madison in the dead of night, tearing at the clothes of a girl I will meet at a party in honour of some momentous retrospective. The driver will be a Hindu and he will laugh hysterically as I slam the Perspex screen shut and instruct him to concentrate on the road. The cab will race through Midtown and on, never stopping where it is supposed to but continuing on through Harlem and all points north to a place of infinite comfort and stability. We will turn the cab into a house, breed and fish regularly, the woman will discard her equality and be free, she will realize that women are superior, after all, and the Hoary Hindu will serve as our factotum; he will keep the meter running until all our children are old enough and rich enough to pay the fare and I will have a boat made for me and Mad Joe to catch the tuna with eyes the size of car headlamps. Everyone and everything will have a place and not even the memory of Elska will block the path of maximum speed, although this is highly doubtful.

Failing all that, I'll go back to Brunmore in Ireland and get a job at Frank the butcher's, which is also the pub.

20

The earnest Englishman called Smythe, who wrote a biography of Dad, once came to ask us questions. I gave him some photographs. He did quite a good job, although I didn't like it when he described me and the other half as "wayward". What the blue blazes does that mean, precisely? He asked Marcello whether he had known Dad well. "No. No one did. He was a good poet."

We're still charging. The last strand of cigarette smoke has struck the ceiling, the girl gone to No Smoking and I don't care either way, about her, about New York, not even about the tuna, for the instant. I look down at the Omega. Enamel Time is ticking along nicely. Everything is working, all is on schedule, slag heap to the left, cars to the right, me in the middle, batteries fully charged, heart beating in time to the second hand. Ahead of us: the tunnel.

After we left the hotel, I bought Elska a drink at the café overlooking the Gardens.

"So, what do we do?"

"We don't do anything," she replied, coolly.

"OK."

"Be realistic, Twist."

"Me?"

"Yes. You."

"No. Kiss me."

"Not here."

"Where?"

"Not anywhere. Look, I have to go. I'm late."

"You went to the movies."

"Fine, we went to the movies."

"No. You went alone to the movies. I never go to the movies. You went to see 'To Have and Have Not'. It's showing down the road."

"I haven't seen it for years."

"You must remember! Lauren Bacall catches Humphrey Bogart carrying a beautiful young woman over to a sofa after she has fainted. Bacall is in love with Bogart and a little jealous, so she says: 'What are you trying to do, Steve? Guess her weight?'"

"I went to the Louvre."

"That's fine. Everyone's been to the Louvre."

"I have to go now."

So she left and she wasn't mine anymore. She was someone else's. I watched her as she walked past the Théâtre de l'Odéon and on, turning the corner into the rue de Tournon. Then I made my way back to the Alabama. Marcello accosted me and got me to come back to his room for a drink. He sat me down in an old armchair and handed me a brass cup of whisky. And he talked. I was content to be led into his world, a world which has taught me how to act, how to disappear at the right moment. And I was grateful for being severed from the turbulence of my afternoon with Elska. I couldn't even think at that point.

"One time, they would pay me to perform magic. I could do many things. I could turn myself into a rabbit and pull myself out of a hat or, with the aid of a fake moustache, pretend to be someone else, reinventing myself in order to earn my keep or to cure a heart which I might have thought was broken.

"I could also do film stars, my favourite being Peter Lorre.

People used to say I looked just like him. That was why I kept a photograph of him in my room, as a joke at my own expense or, in the event I had visitors, at theirs. They would say, 'Is that you?' 'No.' 'Who is it, then?' 'Peter Lorre.' 'But he looks just like you!' 'Everyone looks like someone else. Who do you look like?'

"Yes, they paid me to perform and to look like people. Sometimes, I would turn a member of the audience into the Dead Queen, which was a lot harder to do then than it is now. I couldn't turn her back into a member of the audience, so I asked a member of the audience to stand in for her. This went on for a while, until I had run out of audience. So I turned myself into a member of the audience and applauded. The stage was full of Dead Queens and the promoter was furious.

"That was a long time ago. Afterwards, my agent got me a job in a film, playing the part of a magician. I waited around on set all day, flirting with the make-up girl. In the evening, I was ushered into a corner of the studio and told to start. 'Start what?' I asked. 'You know. Your act. Start!'

"I didn't know what to do. The lights were blinding and my make-up began to drip off in beads of sweat, staining my collar. I had never had stage fright before. The director seemed nervous and tired. I looked ahead at the camera lens and then I looked inside myself, checking to see whether I had any tricks there. But I couldn't find any. Time stopped. Nothing happened. The camera turned and I stared at it vainly.

"It was then that I started to think of a faraway place at the ends of the earth, a spot over the horizon which was full of everything I had ever seen and, at the same time, empty of any frame of reference, a moment trapped in time for ever, a painting which spread beyond its own borders to encompass all that remained unseen. This place – wherever it was – was the meeting of opposites, it was funny and it was not funny, it was empty and it was full, it was sad and it was not sad, it was strange and it was familiar, and I found myself moving within it effortlessly. Yet as soon as I had lost myself to its charms and mysteries, I felt it slipping away from me, like a wave falling back out to sea.

"'That was great!' I heard a voice say, across the gulf that separated me from the camera. 'I like that a lot! Can you do it again for the reverse shot? I mean, exactly what you just did, or as near to it as you can? I mean, it doesn't have to be exactly as you did it, just as near to what you did as you can manage, so we can get in a shot of the audience as you see it? OK?'

"But I hadn't done anything. They wanted me to do exactly what I had done? Or exactly what I hadn't done? When 'Action' was called, I just thought about the faraway place again. I had no idea what I was doing, other than just thinking, that is, but I found I could quite easily slip back into the world I had created for myself. Whatever it was I did, or didn't do, they seemed very pleased with it. As the cameraman and crew applauded, the director rushed forwards and slapped me on the back. 'Give the man a drink or something! He's terrific!'"

21

Everyone has a faraway place to go to. Marcello has his meeting of opposites. Elska has her Metsalämpi, Agostini has his edges and a girl who has learned to cook *pasta al forno*. And me? I have many things, many places, but especially the wandering foam of Yeats, through which I will one day catch my tuna: "*For I would we were changed to white birds on the wandering foam: I and you.*"

I don't need to be a bird, I don't have the head for heights, but I'll take the foam, the wandering foam, swirling around my line as Mad Joe eases the throttle before slipping into neutral.

"We lost him, Joe."

"No we didn't, Twist. He's playing games with you, that's all."

There's a scene in "To Have and Have Not" in which Bogart says much the same thing to an awkward client on his charter boat. It is filmed in a studio so you can see real footage of a marlin leaping in the air behind the players. Mine's not a marlin, but the same sort of film is often played out behind me as I sit here looking through the noughts or lie in Room 76. Bogart was a man of dignity and education. Did he ever read Yeats, I wonder?

The next morning, following my afternoon in the hotel with Elska, I called Flyte. I had to. Silence was an indictment. I wondered how Elska had handled it, but I had no doubt that her sheer imperturbability would save her. Save us. I doubted she would have countenanced our act of betrayal if she had thought, for one second, that she would falter.

"Thanks for lunch, Flyte," I heard myself saying. "You needn't have paid."

"Don't mention it. So, how was it?"

"Fine."

"We should meet before Elska and I go away. Tomorrow, perhaps."

"OK."

I felt far less anxiety than I could have imagined. Hearing Marcello talk of acting had reminded me that that was all I had to do. In fact, it occurred to me suddenly that maybe I should go back to it, just once; it might give me something to do, distract me from Elska. Besides, it was the role I had assigned for myself, was it not?

I wanted to give the impression I was organized and professional and ambitious and it amused me. I called an old producer friend and an agent and arranged to meet them. I had lunch that day with Agostini. I knew he would be enthusiastic, make me do it, even though I was already having second thoughts as I spoke to him.

"Why not? Could be good for you. Got to do something. Your money will run out. Can't just sit in the Alabama dreaming of fish. Look at me. I don't care much for what I do. But it's making me rich. Gets me girls. And you've got to have a girl, haven't you?"

I didn't want to tell Agostini about Elska. Agostini is old school; he might be a wild card, he could break any rule, or any nose, for that matter, but he wouldn't think much of adultery. Even if he could accept the idea, he wouldn't like it, the thought of me and Elska. He was very proprietorial about people. Facing him across that table, I felt his influence and I told myself I should put Elska behind me and forget the whole thing. It became clear to me at that point that I was more apprehensive about him than I was about Flyte. It wasn't because I was afraid of him, it was simply that he made my guilt seem more real.

"I met a girl the other day, called Natasha, from Siberia," he said. "She just arrived in town. She's doing a catalogue. She's got a friend called Eva. Shall we take them out?"

"Sure, Agostini."

I told him about Marcello, whom he had once met. I suggested he take his portrait.

"Where does he come from?"

"The north somewhere."

"Not Veneto. Lombardia?"

"I think so."

"I'll do it."

I have that photograph right in front of me on the unfolded table. Marcello died a month ago, at the end of June, in his sleep. Two days before, he gave me the bound scrapbook with the bits of Dad's poems pasted into it, which Bakir had found under the bed of Room 7. That's the book I'm going to give the other half, when I get to Swallows'. It's all part of the plan. The birthday plan.

22

I met Flyte the following day, in the Café de Flore. Good choice. Either of us was almost bound to meet a friend, or acquaintance, which would prove a distraction if the atmosphere became difficult. As things turned out, I was quite composed. Was it arrogance? Possibly. Or just acting? Better still: the pure abstraction of absurdity.

"So, how was it?"

"Very pleasant. We had a good lunch."

"Elska said she enjoyed it. She must have done. She said she spent the afternoon with you."

I was taken aback slightly. Had she forgotten to tell him she had gone to the Louvre? "She did?"

"Lunch. Gardens. Walk. Must have got on well."

"Well, we've known each other for a long time. It was good to catch up."

"So, what did she tell you?"

"Look, Flyte. She loves you. You know that. Take her away on your vacation. Enjoy being together. Give her a good time. I think Elska's a very private person. You'll just have to accept the fact that you will never really get to know her, because no one will. When do people ever get to know one another, anyway? It's like I said, we just see sides to people. You see a side to Elska I cannot see and I see a side you cannot see. It's like that. Don't expect too much from people. We're all alone, basically. So just allow them to reveal what they want you to see and be satisfied."

"Do you think she's having an affair?"

"So, you did want to know. I told you already she would never tell me, or hint at it, even if she were. Why should she? She doesn't even know me. Don't be so insecure."

"It's not insecurity."

"What is it, then?" I lit a cigarette and glanced around the café. It was busy and there was a lot of noise. I leaned towards him and, as I did so, I thought of *Macbeth* and my favourite line of all, *"There's no art to find the mind's construction in the face."* I certainly couldn't have managed it; the man was a knot of contradictions.

"Look, Flyte, if you try to control something too much, you'll lose it. You'll certainly lose its mystery."

"Mystery? I'm too much of a pragmatist for that."

"No, you're not. You're just kidding yourself. You have poetry in your blood. You can write, which is more than I can."

"You can act."

"Everyone can act. We're acting. Now."

"I'm not much of an actor."

"You're as good as the next man."

We were eating omelettes. Patrick brought us some Bordeaux. Flyte never looked so neat, so accomplished, even the reservations he seemed to have about himself had an order to them. He wore a grey flannel suit and a striped tie that was probably a club, or association; it brought to mind some sophomoric rite of initiation, and I suddenly saw him stark naked jumping into an ice-cold pool at Harvard, applauded by a group of F. Scott Fitzgerald look-alikes. Yes, Flyte had something of Gatsby about him, not so rich, of course, but endowed with the same pretensions to win admiration through apparent generosity.

"Got the college tie on, I see."

"I'm going to a reunion at the Ritz later. Couple of pals have flown over."

"Americans like to keep in touch, don't they? I mean, the college years. You're very sentimental about them. All those alumni get-togethers. What on earth do you find to say to each other apart from 'Do you remember when?'"

"It's our way of belonging, I suppose. America's all about parting. It's the size of the place. Everyone's always getting on a plane. We're rootless."

"You might be rootless. But you're a gentleman, Flyte. An upright. Be comfortable with yourself!" I couldn't believe I was saying this. It was like reading from a script. "As far as Elska is concerned, she wants to be with you, otherwise she wouldn't be with you. It's as simple as that."

"Are you attracted to her?"

"Elska's a beautiful woman."

"So what else did she tell you?"

"Oh, we just chatted. You know how it is. I'd no idea she was half Finnish."

"Half Dutch."

"We're all a mixture, are we not?" I continued blindly. "It's like America. You've got Irish-Americans and American-Indians, probably even got Irish-Indians by now. How about that? An Irish-Indian! What a nutter he'd be, charging around with a squaw in one hand and a shillelagh in the other."

Agostini had appeared. Right on cue. "What's a shillelagh?"

"It's an Irish club."

"Any good?"

"No. A club, you know. A stick. For beating people up."

"Sit down, Agostini. If you wish," said Flyte, rising to shake his hand.

"I don't want to derange you."

"Disturb, Agostini. Disturb," said Flyte. "You're not, anyway. Have a drink."

So, the three of us sat and talked about the emptiness of Paris now that August had taken over.

"You going away? With Elska?" asked Agostini.

"In a few days. Spain and Portugal."

"What's wrong with Naples? You can stay in my place. Maybe you wouldn't like it. Good food, though."

Patrick brought Agostini a drink and the three of us clinked glasses. Flyte looked perturbed, all of a sudden. "You weren't planning on killing Jean-Pierre, were you, Agostini?"

"Of course not." Agostini smiled. "Guess what? Twist is going to be an actor again."

"Is that true, Twist?"

"I'm thinking about it."

"Even though you never go to the cinema?"

"You don't go to the cinema to act. You go to watch."

"Well, I'm glad everything's smoothed over as far as Jean-Pierre is concerned. Elska's rather fond of him."

"Bit of an idiot though, isn't he?" said Agostini.

Flyte looked at him. Then at me. He smiled in a way I had never seen him smile before. There was very little New World about it. It was deeply sardonic. Was he onto me?

"Of course!" he said, taking a swig of wine and shrugging his shoulders plaintively.

23

Elska did not try to contact me before they left. I waited those three days and nights. But there was nothing, not a sign from her. It would have been so easy for her. A note at the Alabama. A telephone call. A letter. I can't say I was particularly surprised. She obviously thought the whole thing was a mistake.

"Be realistic," she had said. Realistic?

I still didn't understand what was going on, not even a fraction of it. And, on the day they left for Iberia, five days after my lunch with Flyte at the Café de Flore, I found myself standing on the balcony at the Alabama, staring out at Paris in anger. I doubted, at that point, whether I would see either of them again. They were both behaving so strangely and, in that respect, probably deserved each other. But who was I to interfere, or even have an opinion? They were a married couple. I had no right to be angry about anything. I had started something I wasn't supposed to have done. Hadn't I?

Perhaps I should have left Paris then? I had money, after all. I could have gone to Long Island, it was the season for it. I could have gone to Rio. I could have gone anywhere. The Philippines have seven thousand one hundred islands and a friend, now dead, once wrote me a letter from one of them, to tell me of a pretty girl he had met and a house he had rented on stilts. He was murdered in Paris, they blew up his flat and all that the *sapeurs* found afterwards were his teeth, lying in the gutter. But I have the letter he sent me, I carry it around with me and it's a good letter, it speaks of another world and, when I think of him, I see him walking along the sand with his girl, who was probably a damned fine cook, as well as everything else. Was it time to head East for a change?

No. I wasn't about to leave. I don't mind running when I have to. But here there was no reason to. I'd just returned. It would be stupid. I determined to forget about Elska, pretend it never happened. Had it ever happened at all? I found myself saying, as I looked over the rooftops and down at the market, at the tourists questioning the price of a banana or the way to the nearest bureau de change. Paris, such an easy accommodator of memory, heartache and illusion, even if, as Agostini's glossy magazines stated, less happened than it used to.

There was no work, no acting, which was fine. It was August. Actors planning a comeback could do no worse than choose the dead month. I drifted. And read. One evening, Marcello showed me a couple of letters Dad had sent him when he was away, on a lecture tour in America. They were from the middle Sixties and I was fascinated by them, as much by the fact that I could see myself then, eight or nine years old, tramping off to school at Jussieu with the other half and fighting in the playground, as by the voice of my father that spoke to me from so far away.

Everything was tinged in shades of grey in those letters, those accounts from the modern world of America. They sent him all over the place, to universities in the Midwest and institutes for learned societies in the South, and Dad was funny about it all. "They've been asking me, at question time, whether I suffer much as a poet. I think they like their poets and artists to suffer. It makes sense to them. For a few extra dollars I'd tell them I starved as an infant, but I'm on a fixed rate so I tell them I was brought up in a suite at the Shelbourne Hotel. Shocks the mainstream but goes down well with the corporate types. For all that, this is a great place, mapfuls of space to get lost in and a bar on every corner. Keep an eye on Brenda but one only."

One day, Moraes called me and instructed me to come to Rio. I thought about it. I didn't mention Elska. But I knew he suspected something. Moraes and I have an understanding akin to that which binds me and the other half, a telepathy of sorts. We don't talk very much, we never need to. It is the absence of dialogue which counts, which makes the difference. Conrad talked about this mystery in one of his books. He said that an island was just the peak of a mountain surrounded by water. Why does everyone want to dive to the bottom?

These were empty days and I passed many of them alone, quietly, catching my breath. I thought about myself, who I was, what I was, and I realized that my feelings for all that is inexplicable are what make me, they are a part of me, as natural as tea and biscuits on a lawn in summer. They have never left me, they constitute my faith, my intuition, so that I hardly nod when faced with the strangest coincidence, the most perfect and absurd happenstance. In the cyclical, seasonal, resurrectional rhythms that have accompanied my walking, waking life, I have never doubted the beauty, wonder and fragile refinements of existence, a leaf falling through space and caught as if for the first time, no matter how many million leaves I have seen slip to the floor of memory, my spirit soars and I note, subconsciously, the transference of one being to another with the same beguiling wonderment. My telepathy takes the form of an invisible line, electrically charged, connecting my intuition with that of my other half, that split cell which, forty years and nine months ago, turned in the womb from a microscopic reflection into a sparring partner, exasperating the mammy with ten round bouts and knockout punches as she sallied forth into the supermarket of her pregnancy.

My other half. Moraes. Agostini. Marcello, even dead. Even Flyte, after all that has happened, all that has been revealed. A Confederacy of Uprights lost within a crowd of humanity that struggles to prove more happens in one place than in another. The world spins, I pick it up, toss it into the air and stare at it. Not a bad place to end up in, given there's no choice in the matter.

I walked the streets, I chatted to the *garçons* in the bars and I watched the dawn break, repeatedly, as if trying to do a better job than the day before, with a bit more colour maybe. You can't beat the dawn, it proves you're still alive; every day is another chance to do some business or other.

One night I dreamed I was in front of the camera, as Marcello had been. I couldn't learn my lines, I had had a drink and the words refused to lodge themselves within me. I cursed them, those elusive lines which so tormented my powers of recall, but, when the time came, I found them with ease; I didn't have to think, they were there all the time, I wasn't thinking at all, I was merely acting. A fine actor from Albion was once asked what the secret to the job was. "Just pretend," he said. So that's what I did, even as I slept.

24

Then, one day towards the end of August, I was walking past the Cinematone cinema when I saw the short film advertised. The poster was very subtle and blurred but you could just make out an arm, or a leg, which must have been Elska's. Imagine that! Elska's arm or leg stuck on a wall in the rue des Écoles for all to see! Sure enough, it had the director's name on it in large lettering, for the French always make a song and a dance about the director, just as they make a song and a dance about hairdressers.

LA DERNIÈRE GOUTTE. JEAN-PIERRE CORTANZE.

That was it. No actors or anything. Just a picture of a part of Elska and the fellow's name with the title: "The Last Drop". Drinking? Or parachuting? I hesitated for a moment. Then I bought myself a ticket and a can of beer and went in.

I used to go to the movies all the time. And then I stopped, because I was tired of acting and the whole thing. There was no hope of being a poet because I couldn't follow in the footsteps and I wasn't a poet in the first place. Never have been. Someone who wasn't Irish once told me that all the Irish are poets, which is not really true if you think about it, although I would say that all poets are Irish, or Italian maybe. Who's to say, and me the last, what poetry is or isn't, anyway? I never had much of a clue. So I acted. It was the nearest thing I could think of to tiger-taming. And it had to be better than joining the bloody Legion, taking pot shots at a bunch of African-Africans and getting blown up like poor Myles.

"The Last Drop"! Well, it wasn't such a bad film. Certainly had its moments. Elska was fascinating in it. She had to play the part, even though she played herself, of a woman who is abandoned by the fellow we all reckoned was an idiot but who, surprisingly, knew how to act. He was completely different in front of the camera; it didn't even look like him, he'd had a shave and he was far more sincere and interesting in the part than he was railing against Hollywood and telling us that Amsterdam was like Venice, but in the north.

So he goes off with someone else, a blonde he meets in a bar, but then she leaves him in turn, so he returns to Elska, contrite. But she's gone, the man realizes his mistake too late and he will spend the rest of his life in love with a memory, a shadow. The end sees him reading a letter from Elska in which she anticipated everything from the beginning, right down to the last detail. She wasn't in love with him, she was using him to get over someone else, before. And she tells him as much in the letter. Nice touch, I thought. "Revenge is a meal best served cold," as the Arabs like to say.

It's a silly enough story but the film is not just a story, it's more of a clever jumble of still-lives and words spoken over them, words which don't correspond to the pictures but which either anticipate or review them. Elska's voice carried me on a wave somewhere and every time she appeared on screen I was enthralled and mystified by her ambiguity, so analogous to her real self which, of course, is what she is in the film. Passive throughout, abstracted from circumstances, which she accepts with resignation, she is both above and beyond it all and, when we see her at the end, on the bank of a lake on the edge of a forest, we realize that whatever happened to her is of no real consequence.

Throughout the film, she is not the subject but the object of desire, an observer, experimenting with life and people, propelled exclusively by her curiosity. Perfect! Jean-Pierre was not, after all, such an idiot. He had made a complete portrait of the woman. Should have won a prize or a medal or something.

They always say you can't have a good film without a good script, so this film with a bad script is the exception, saved by Elska. Watching her close-up on the large screen of the Cinematone, expressionless, caught in some unfathomable moment of introspection, her eyes impassive, her lips stilled, her voice carried over, I was teased into thinking I was actually alone with her, a pardonable delusion given the fact I was the only person in the auditorium. The love-making scene, preposterous as it was, took my breath away, her nudity all the more tantalizing for being partially disguised and flattened into two dimensions. That back! That is what the film was about. God alone knows why the man called it "La Dernière Goutte". Should have been "Elska's Back".

I saw it seven times that week. I cannot honestly state it helped me to forget Elska.

25

I longed to be with Elska after watching that film. I was powerless. I just waited. I thought of Myles when he went AWOL. He arrived home at the flat on rue Monge and sat in his room, reading Dad's poetry and staring up at the ceiling. And then, after a few days, he appeared in the kitchen in his uniform.

"I'm off now. Going back. They'll find me sooner or later. So, it's better this way. They'll stick me in the slammer for a month, but I don't regret it. It was worth it, to see you."

We never saw him again and, when I think of him, I always think of him standing there, with his kitbag. Why did he have to go and join up? I curse the day Dad and the mammy took us to watch the Legionnaires marching down the Champs-Elysées with their aprons and axes, for it was that *defilé* that inspired him, just as the circus and the tigers inspired me.

I wasn't as badly off as Myles, but there's something universal about lying in your room alone trying to make up your mind what to do. You kid yourself you're being objective, you act the part of your own devil's advocate in order to give substance to your decision, but your intuition has already settled the issue beforehand. Such is life, and all the prevarication in the world doesn't make the slightest scrap of difference. Myles knew he'd go back before he left. If only we had realized we could have forced him to stay, against his wishes if necessary, and, by so doing, saved him. That's why the mammy never got over it. Dad wrote a poem but he never showed it to anyone. I think he threw it away. I asked Marcello about it when he gave me the scrapbook.

"Your father never mentioned a poem. But, like Brenda, he never came to terms with it."

I tried to distract myself as best I could; from Elska, from the past, the teeth of sadness. Agostini came back from a trip, so we went out. After a couple of drinks, I was on the point of telling him about it all. I checked myself. Then I said I'd met a girl, but she was with someone. I needed to hear what he'd say.

"Just take her. Go and get her. Be done with it. If you're in love, there's no other way. Don't expect anyone to understand. It's between you and her. No one else."

"What about her partner?"

"That's his problem. He's probably done something wrong. And she's not in love with him if she wants to be with you."

"Can't be that simple, Agostini. Nothing is ever that simple."

"Come non? Non c'è niente di più facile dell'amore! Cazzo!"

This was a mistake. I needed someone to tell me to forget about Elska, not encourage me. Someone to oppose my instincts. Like one of the fathers at school, a couple of Hail Marys, ten francs in the box and off to a new dawn. Well, it wasn't going to be like that.

Agostini had arranged the double date he'd been talking about. He was very excited; he said Natasha was a beauty and that I could have Eva, who wasn't bad either. We met in a restaurant and went to a club afterwards. Eva was all over me, Agostini must have told her I was a modelling agent or something, but I couldn't summon up the interest. I wanted to take my revenge on Elska, but my heart wasn't in it. What I really felt was that I was betraying her, which only proved to me how deluded I had become. I left them to it and Agostini ended up with both of them. He called me the next morning.

"*O stess' moment' tutt'e dduie russe pazzariell'!*" he screamed. "Was desperate. Like being on the raft of the Medusa!"

August dragged its heels. A friend called Walter showed up for the weekend. He used to live in Paris. Then he went back to Vienna. I met him in a bar in the Bastille. He was with a woman I had never met before, whom he introduced as an old friend. I knew Walter was married so I assumed they were just that: friends.

The woman was attractive in an oblique way and she had a sense of humour. I can't remember where she came from. We went from bar to bar and finally came across a club where they played salsa music. I started dancing with the woman; it was hot, we sweated, and Walter stood up at the counter smiling, trying to persuade the barman to give us free drinks.

We danced closer and closer and started kissing and, as we kissed, Elska slipped out of my mind for a moment. This went on for a while. We went to another place, then another and it was four o'clock in the morning and I was kissing her against a tree on a street corner while Walter stayed in the bar. Suddenly, she drew away from me.

"What's the matter?" I asked.

"Is this a set-up?"

"What do you mean?"

"It's Walter."

"What are you talking about?"

"We're supposed to be together. Is he trying to palm me off or something?"

I was shocked. I had no idea she was Walter's girlfriend. He hadn't given any sign. But she was in love with him, it was suddenly very obvious. Then why was she kissing me? To make him jealous? I wasn't forcing myself on her. Not at all.

"I had better speak to him."

"Please don't," she said.

"Wait here."

I went into the bar and found him. "Walter! I didn't realise."

"Realise what?"

"About you and the girl. That you were together."

"Don't worry, Twist. You can have her. You're a friend."

I was drunk. I went back outside and found her. She was standing, quite still, beside the tree, smoking a cigarette.

"It's fine," I said, stupidly. "Walter doesn't mind."

"Well, I do."

"You're trying to make him jealous. Is that the idea? I mean, what's going on, exactly?"

I walked away, in disgust. I was beginning to develop a complex. First Elska. Now this. It bruised me. Walter had set me up, he'd enjoyed it all, he'd made a fool of me and he'd made a fool of the girl. And there he was, leaning against the bar inside, smiling to himself as we kissed.

I think I realized then, more than at any other time, just how tricky love can be. That it can become a weapon if you want it to. Agostini was wrong, quite wrong. Love wasn't simple. Not simple at all. The feeling might be, but the way people used it wasn't.

I went back to the Alabama. I stood on my balcony. I sighed, deeply, and inhaled the good and the bad air of Paris and I saw chaos below me, something that was not always perfectly enchanting.

26

Flyte and Elska were due back at the beginning of September. I didn't know which day exactly but, as August finally ended, I knew it could be any time, any minute. Flyte would call me sooner or later and I decided to wait. I had no idea whether Elska would try to contact me. Prayed she would, prayed she wouldn't.

In the mean time, another tense altogether, I got a job on a film. The agent I had called contacted me; he said the person they had lined up for the part had dropped out of the project and that I should take it. I went to the casting. For once, I prepared myself as if my life depended on it, which was ironic enough, as it was the only time in my life I didn't need the money. I barked my lines, for the scene demanded anger on occasion, and, when I had finished, the casting director coughed and was silent for a while.

"You have a great deal of energy," she said. "Too much perhaps. But you're good. We'll call you."

I desperately wanted that role, I thought it might solve everything somehow, I thought it might change me, rekindle an interest in something other than Elska and tuna fish and getting drunk with Agostini and thinking about the past. I was wrong, of course. As soon as I showed up on set I couldn't have given a damn about it.

The film was a gangster love story and it was set around

Paris. I was a hired hand. They asked me whether I had ever handled a gun and they gave me a .357 Magnum. I once fired a Magnum in Mad Joe's garden. It's big and heavy and it takes over your character like a false beard or a forced limp, becoming a part of you. You pull out that great weight of nastiness, your hand feels heavy and you know you can be more unpleasant than you could ever have imagined. I don't need a gun to be unpleasant but, with a Magnum, I don't even have to try.

In one of the scenes, I had to wait in the getaway car outside a bank in Neuilly. A man notices me. And there I am, in the car with my Magnum. I don't know whether the man is a cop or entirely innocent and, as he walks towards where I am parked, waiting for my partners to come out of the bank and cross the street, I have to decide what to do. He steps up to the car and I open the window.

"Mind your own business! Or I'll kill you!"

That's my line in the scene. "Mind your own business! Or I'll kill you!" The man puts his hand inside his jacket and I realize he is a cop, so I shoot him with the Magnum and there he is, with a hole in him, lying dead on the pavement. The others come out with the money and get into the car and I drive off.

Of course, I should have known better. I should have known that pretending to kill someone in a movie wasn't going to help in any way. It was certainly not going to help me forget Elska. It would have taken a thousand gangster films and even then it wouldn't have made any difference. It's like that. Love. That's what I have learned.

During the filming, I would return to the Alabama, hoping to find a message. But there wasn't one. This went on for three weeks or more. I felt empty inside, empty of all hope, and I carried on my work routinely, hardly believing what I was doing. On the last day, when we wrapped, I got back to the hotel very late. Wolf was there, rolling a cigarette.

Elska had called. Was I interested in dinner?

Part Five
TRIPE

27

Everything is an illusion. Even that evening with Walter and his friend, who tried to make him jealous by allowing me to kiss her but who maybe didn't want that, after all. Maybe she wasn't really in love with Walter, maybe she actually wanted me, maybe she wasn't Walter's to give away and Walter was just making it up because he didn't think the truth would come out, whatever that is or was? Who knows and it's too late to ask now? I don't give a damn anyway, I'm on this train and it is all behind me, like a dirty hotel room you pay for and forget about as soon as you step out into the street.

We'll soon be entering the tunnel. The tunnel, the whole nothingness, the noting of absence, the void, the life without love or light. My window will stop being something to look through, it will become an impenetrable mirror tinted with sadness, just as that train in Africa somewhere is tinted with gold, and all I will see is my own, tired face, asking endless questions of itself.

I look up from the definitive *Life of Twist* to find the girl sitting opposite me. She has returned and I didn't even notice. We attend to the same ritual: she puts her cigarette to her lips and I light it for her. When she now looks in the window, her reflection is sharper than before, I can see it quite clearly from the corner of my eye as I continue the business of scribbling, her eye blinks, she brings the cigarette to her lips and smoke rises through the glass, grey, white almost, without a hint of blue. She knows I am looking at her. And there she sits, quietly smoking and staring. She turns to me and I stop the writing, right where it is, here, at this bit of enamel.

"You can stay here if you want. I mean, the seat's not taken. Save you going backwards and forwards all the time."

She smiles. "I don't need to. Thanks all the same," she says, with a strong accent. I knew she was French. From the start. Why did I speak to her in English? Why did I speak to her at all? I didn't want to enter into conversation. I never do that when I'm travelling. It's such an absurd thing to do, once you've started, you've had it, there's no going back and, even if you stop talking, the silence is filled with even more expectation than it was before.

"Vous voyagez avec quelqu'un qui ne fume pas? C'est ça?"

"Yes," she answers.

"A man?"

"Yes."

"Husband?" I sound like passport control.

"No."

"Lover?"

"No. Friend."

"A friend who'd like to be your lover but who doesn't like smoke?"

"Perhaps."

"Wouldn't surprise me. You're a good-looking girl."

"Thanks."

I can't believe I'm doing this, having a conversation with a girl on the train, here, in Enamel Time, we haven't even got to the tunnel yet and I'm nowhere near finishing my Linear Composition in Solitude Management, I've still got to sleep with Elska a dozen more times before the story's stopped, the circle's turning well but we still have more turning to do, and diverting myself like this is not helping the process one bit; I'm condemned now, condemned to the expectancy of chatter, cutting it off now will make me look ridiculous and rude, not to put too fine a point on it. I don't want to be rude, I just want to be left to myself. It's my own fault.

I put my hand in my pocket, looking for another box of matches. I feel the packet of condoms, I look at the girl and my imagination leaps like an excited finger over the edge of the wrapper. What am I doing? I take another miniature of Martell and unscrew it. I push it across the table with a smile. This time, she takes it.

"Thanks."

She sips from the bottle, smarting at the contents, until the last drop, *la dernière goutte,* is gone. She puts the empty bottle back on the table. A man, who must be her companion, now appears from behind me and leans over her. I put the headphones of the Walkman back onto my head and I watch as she frowns at the man, pointing to her cigarette. I look up. The man seems perturbed for some reason. He looks at me derisively and then marches back up the carriage. The girl smiles at me. Don't tell me she prefers me to him simply because I smoke? How cock-eyed is that? I feel the condoms in my pocket again. Then I pick up my pencil and begin writing. The girl has now stubbed out her cigarette. Looking up, I smile at her. Then I take off the headphones and place them carefully over her head, before continuing my scribbling, I am now in a state of complete, unadulterated comfort and stability, I have stopped and started and stopped and started and all that remains is for me to carry on doing what I have to do and get back to Elska. At the same time, I ask myself whether life will ever stop falling into my lap; will it, just for once, get stuck in the enamel long enough for me to get it all down on paper?

28

Yes, I am just doing what I have to do in order to set the record straight and stop time in its tracks for a moment.

Where was I? Going out to dinner. Slowing up for the tunnel. Now I am *in* the tunnel, it came forward to meet us all halfway, as I had imagined it would. The train has finally put some brakes on and everything is different now. We've gone from maximum speed to maximum darkness and this great monster feels somehow impotent all of a sudden, reduced to nothing more than its potential.

I look up. The girl has removed the headphones and gone. I didn't even notice her departure. I turn to the window. It has become a mirror and I don't like it, I don't want to see those sunken eyes, those retinae eclipsed by curved, concrete walls, I want to be up, up above, on a boat crashing through the foam, *"the wandering foam"*, falling into a trough as it heads north, or south, or wherever it wishes, I want to feel a gale try to push me around as I grasp a stanchion, I want to bring Elska close to me, closer, closer, so that her hair whips the side of my face. I protect her even though she never needs protection, even though she has said she needs no help from a man. Damn her! Bless her!

The dinner. Agostini was absent, taking pictures somewhere, so there would be no one to ride shotgun for me this time. I was alone, yet I told myself I was simply going to sit opposite a woman with whom I had once slept, that was all. No harm in that. I could hardly refuse. Could I?

I was the last to arrive. Flyte and Elska were standing by the mantelpiece, an elephant each; Kajfa was seated, perfectly relaxed, in an armchair; and a man I had never met before sat on the sofa. Flyte introduced me to the stranger: he was one of his friends from New York, an editor called Thorpe.

"Evening, Thorpe!"

Elska looked exactly the same. She always looked the same; nothing, not the slightest detail, ever changed. And she gave nothing away as I kissed her on the cheek, my heart falling beneath me to the eminently tasteful rug, its pattern a swirling parody of drunkenness, a forest for me and the elephants to get lost in, my brown boots planted in its undergrowth with resolution and defiance as I struggled with that hardest act of all: normality.

Elska disappeared into the kitchen. I shook Thorpe's hand. "Seamus O'Leary. But everyone calls me Twist. No idea why. Think it was Dad's idea. Originally."

Thorpe was the charming sort, handsome, willowy: shock of blond hair, gold-rimmed spectacles, starched shirt, shoes you could have eaten off. He was already trying his hand with Kajfa. Would he succeed where Jean-Pierre had failed, Jean-Pierre, now an esteemed and upright genius as a result of his *chef-d'oeuvre*, "Elska's Back"? I doubted it.

"Amsterdam? An interesting city," he exclaimed, making it quite clear that I had, by being late, upset the disorder and interrupted his opening gambit.

"All cities are interesting, are they not?" she replied.

"You'll have to do better than that, Thorpe." I took my drink from Flyte, who revealed a smile of uncertain provenance.

"But Kayfer..."

"It's Ky-fer, John. Spelt K-A-J-F-A. But pronounced Ky-fer." Flyte's explanation summarized the cultural challenge of Europe in two syllables.

"Ky-fer. Ky-fer was telling me she came from Amsterdam. I'd like to go."

"You don't really need to, do you? I mean, Amsterdam came to you."

"Don't start being difficult, Twist," Flyte said, still smiling.

"Where do you come from, Twist?" asked Thorpe.

"Ireland."

"I've heard it's become quite the place at the moment."

"At the moment?"

"Have you been, Gerald?" asked Thorpe. It was strange hearing Flyte called by his first name. Made him seem like another person.

"Twist never invited me."

"I don't go anymore. I was born here. We used to visit, all of us, now and then. The mammy came from Brunmore. Dad from Dublin. Originally."

"The mammy?"

"My mother. An affectation. Traditional usage."

"I see."

"And you, Thorpe? New York? Just visiting?"

"Yes. We have some authors here. Wasn't your father a poet?"

"That's what he called himself. That's what he was. A poet."

"I know his American publisher."

"He's dead, actually. He died fifteen years ago. The mammy died a fortnight later. There's just me and the other half now."

"The other half?"

"My twin."

Flyte suggested we take our places. I sat between Flyte and Kajfa, who presently reappeared from the kitchen with an enormous bowl of pasta. Thorpe was opposite me, Elska between him and Kajfa. Insidious oval!

I was wrong about Elska. She was very slightly different from before. I couldn't quite pinpoint how, because I was too busy trying to distract myself with conversation, listening to Thorpe as he embarked on an abridged autobiography which had already awarded him a Rhodes scholarship by the time the first ladle of gnocchi had been deposited on my plate. I found myself glancing at Elska repeatedly and finally burst out, "You've lost weight, Elska. You're thinner. Too thin. What have you been doing?"

"Have I?"

Thorpe had returned to America and already written his first novel. No one was listening to us.

"Yes."

A period of wandering, or wondering. Suddenly we are in Los Angeles, the dreaded Hollywood threatens to submerge young Thorpe's talents.

"I've been exercising."

"Not weights, I hope."

Elska laughed. "Swimming, mostly."

Rejecting Hollywood because of its "value system", the intrepid Thorpe now settles in New York. One evening, he meets Andy Warhol. He becomes part of the "Downtown Scene". Must have been the early Eighties. Good. Only sixteen years to go.

"John published one or two of my stories," added Flyte, modestly. "Bravely edited, I must say."

"Not a bit of it, Gerald. I hardly touched them."

Now disowning the "rampant capitalism" and "seditious art market" of the period, Thorpe, carelessly bypassing Flyte's literary endeavours, rattles through the seasons like an incoming Local and takes us all the way up, all the way down, to the present. We are now in the picture. Kajfa looked on, bewildered by the comprehensiveness of the monologue. Flyte smiled approvingly. The humour of it all relaxed me and I found myself simply content to be in Elska's company.

"Flyte's a good writer. I keep on telling him. Glad you agree," I said to Thorpe.

"He certainly is."

"Tell him to do more of it."

"I have done."

The meal progressed without incident. Afterwards, we drank port, then coffee and Cognac, and Thorpe became visibly drunk, slurring his words and then, finally, closing up, as if there were nothing more to say, which may well have been the case. Suddenly, he rose from the table and, losing all those hard-won, adult years in one faltering step, suggested a dance with Kajfa, by whom he was clearly fascinated. She consented and soon they were engaged in a kind of dismal smooch, which was mildly embarrassing to the others, who were not sure whether or not to join in. I saw my chance and took Elska's hand, while Flyte busied himself in his study, looking for a book, or a bottle.

Dancing with Elska, holding her lightly at the waist, feeling her so near to me, my senses consumed by her scent and by the touch of her skin, I was transported back to the hotel room. I was filled with the inexpressible joy that she still wanted to see me and that was all I cared about. Thankfully, everyone had had a great deal to drink by this stage, so my rapture remained private, for it must have showed, somehow, even if it was not noticed.

We were apart from the others. I moved my head brazenly to her ear and whispered, "I love you, Elska!", and she pulled away and gave me the most quizzical expression imaginable.

"Ssssshhh!" she whispered. "Sssssshhhhhhhh!"

Thorpe had disentangled himself from Kajfa and gone into

Flyte's study, which left me dancing with Elska, while Kajfa looked on from the dining table, drinking a glass of port and looking radiant, almost smug.

When Flyte and Thorpe returned to the room, I was at the table again, pouring myself a drink, and Elska and Kajfa had their backs to the mantel, chatting excitedly, their laughter growing louder and louder as they egged each other on with some preposterous tale. This left me with the two men and we looked at the volumes Flyte had brought in from his study. There was one of Dad's, *Poems for the Dead and a Living*, numbered and signed.

"It's a good one," I said. "He wrote it at the Alabama. *'Hush twinkle, twin chuckle.'*"

"Where's that one? I don't remember it."

"It's not there. I just made it up for some reason," I said. Then I shook hands with them, kissed the girls and said good-bye. It was an abrupt enough departure. But acting is not something you can do indefinitely.

29

I called Flyte and Elska the next morning to thank them for the dinner. My chances were even that Elska would answer. If Flyte answered, I would suggest we meet for lunch, make a few acerbic comments about Thorpe and perhaps ask Flyte why Americans always behave as if they are being interviewed for a job when you first meet them. Something like that, anyway. Just to up the ante.

And if Elska answered? We had to meet. As soon as possible. It was simple. I can think of few advantages, moral or practical, to conducting an affair with a friend's partner. But at least calling is not a problem. Hello, Flyte? What's up?

It was Elska. She agreed to meet me a few days later in the café on the other side of the Gardens, for lunch.

It was getting colder; we were already well into October. Elska's hair was up, tied with the silver pin, and she wore a black coat and grey scarf. Time was playing tricks, the change in the seasons gave our love a new dimension, a cycle had begun of which I was not fully aware but which had a certain inevitability to it, as if it were the narrative thread to a story. One doesn't have to be a mystic to take note of such things. Beginnings always presuppose endings and, while love affairs, generally speaking, are easier to start than conclude, they always hold, within their peculiar dynamic, the promise of a tidy narrative structure, as if they were being or had been constructed by some keen, not always gifted observer. A writer, perhaps.

One's life may, or may not, have been invented before being acted out. Coincidences, interfering, colluding with destiny, only confirm the fact. Destiny? Odd word. Sounds pompous and mock-heroic in English, yet banal, almost meaningless, in French. The English are apprehensive about the word, because it implies a grandeur they would rather stifle with modesty and understatement, while the French use it with an abandon that undervalues it, simultaneously justifying its existence and relegating it to a cliché.

And the Irish? We talk less of destiny. It is as if, through the desperate nature of our history, we had once been blessed with it and subsequently, through strife, robbed of it. With destiny reduced and elevated to myth, we plod forth into the night, gormless, drunk and ranting. "Ireland," said Dad. "Nothing green about it, it's red and bloody and bloody hopeless."

Destiny! Elska appearing in the doorway of the café twenty minutes late (she was always so reliable in her tardiness), the gangster actor, now cast as a cad, rising from the table and walking into an embrace, holding her, feeling the chill to her cheeks, kissing her on the lips. Perfect shot, first take. How natural things are when you don't have to think of them, when you forget the script and allow pure, animal, tiger instinct to take over!

"Thank God for autumn," she said. "I love it. Leaves falling. Clear sky. And winter, too. The summer was so hot. Too hot."

"What are we going to do, Elska?"

"We're doing it." Kind smile, hasty. "Let's not talk. Why talk about it? Men always want to discuss everything, have answers, they are like children. Flyte's just the same. All men are the same."

"You're angry."

"Perhaps."

We ordered. "So, how is Flyte?" I asked, breaking my own promise not to discuss him. I was too keen to find out what was going on.

"We fought. On holiday. Now it's better."

"He doesn't know, does he?"

"Of course not."

"Perhaps he's frustrated. You know what he's like. He should be writing. I was horrified to learn he was working for the glossy magazines. He doesn't need to. He can do what he wants. He's a writer. Is it insecurity? Or what?"

"I don't know."

"I can understand modesty. But not that. I'll have to have a word with him."

"You should. He respects you."

"We've got to stick together. Art is sacred. Flyte is able to observe and he has technique, he knows how to put words together so they sound right. Why does he hang out with people like Thorpe and the others? He's way above them."

"You're just saying this because you feel guilty. You'd never have felt so strongly about his work if you hadn't slept with me."

"That's not it. Art is separate."

"Nonsense. But you can delude yourself, if it pleases you. If it makes you feel better."

"We all delude ourselves. It's in our nature. But it's different with poetry. You don't understand my upbringing. We practically starved for the old man's sake."

"Your father was a great poet."

"Great or not. It's all the same in the end."

"You should have been a poet, Twist."

"It's not a job. You've got to know what you're doing. And I don't. None of us was meant to follow in the footsteps. Except Myles. Maybe that's what he would have done if he hadn't got himself killed."

"You always talk about him. Is it terrible for you?"

"Yes. And no. I never got over it. But then, I never got over a lot of things. Just learned to live with them."

"Is that why you act? In order to deal with everything?"

"Probably. It wasn't really my idea. Dad thought it up. I think the idea amused him. I lost interest in it. I mean, what's the point?"

"You just did a film, didn't you?"

"I was a gangster. I had to shoot someone."

"Did you enjoy it?"

"Shooting someone? Yes I did actually. Myles told me once, when he went AWOL, that he'd shot someone. In Chad or somewhere near to it. He was on guard duty and there was a riot. Gave the man a burst of fire and killed him on the spot. He always thought he would pay for it. He did."

We drank our wine in silence for a moment and watched the rain and the leaves coming down and looked at the people scurrying about, getting wet and seeking shelter in the doorway of the café. I turned to Elska.

"Did I tell you I saw the film? You were beautiful. Stole the show. I saw it seven times."

"So, you changed your mind about Jean-Pierre?"

"Not really. But I changed my mind about you."

"How so?"

"I thought I could forget about you. While you were away. Then I realised how much I loved you. I do love you."

"Because of the film?"

"Not exactly."

"It's an easy thing to say, isn't it? 'I love you'?"

"Not really. At least, I'm not in the habit of it."

We finished our lunch and went for a walk in the Gardens. I asked Elska whether she had told Flyte we were meeting and, when she said she hadn't, I felt a shiver go down my spine. I don't know why I should have found that so shocking but, in many ways, it was the true beginning of deceit, even more decisive, somehow, than making love with Elska in the hotel in July.

It was done. We were caught. And we went back to the hotel to repeat, in a different way, what we had done before. Of all the levellers, all the diversions, all the escapes, all the diversions into amnesia, sex surely ranks first place. And, with Elska, it was never anything else.

30

We met again. And again. Same café. Same walk. Just more leaves everywhere as the days shortened.

We talked less and less. In fact, we soon found ourselves performing our affair, as if it was something above and beyond us. It had a character to it endowed with a strange innocence. We would meet in the café, skipping lunch, meeting at three o'clock, drinking a glass of champagne and walking through the Gardens back to the hotel on the rue de Médicis. Soon, we were meeting at the café at the bottom of the street, a few doors down from the hotel, encouraged by the entirely absurd notion of saving time. Saving time? Time isn't something you can save until it's past, or locked in the memory box.

"What are you thinking?" I asked her, on the sixth occasion, as we lay apart upon the bed, smoking cigarettes.

"I think we should stop this."

"Because it's too difficult?"

"Partly."

"Because you're in love with Flyte?"

"That's got nothing to do with it."

"Well, it's hardly a detail. It must be hard for you having to describe non-existent exhibitions to him all the time."

"No. I always went out a lot. Seeing people. Doing things. It's not that."

"So? What is it?"

"It's good. I enjoy it. But..."

"You *enjoy* it. Is that all? Like going to the movies?"

"No. If it were like going to the movies, then that is what I'd do. It would be a lot less complicated. I wouldn't have to feel so terrible when I climb the stairs in rue Jacob. Would I?"

It suddenly occurred to me that we were killing it already. Once you start talking about something, it's over. Especially an affair. I had thought it strange that we had said so little during the previous times we had met. And now I saw how precious that was. Not talking, just being together, bound by all that was unsaid. It was like that poem Dad wrote once, in which he constructs a picture in negative: *"From all the absence noted..."*

"Well?" I said, stubbing out my cigarette and turning to her, propping myself on one elbow and drawing a strand of hair away from her cheek. "That's great, isn't it? You said you didn't want to talk about it. And now you do. Because it's too late, we've lost something, whatever it is, and you've decided it can't be retrieved."

Was it, I wondered, the initial excitement of transgression? Had habit crept into our love and gnawed away at it, as habit always does, slowly destroying precious things like a cancer?

"It's not too late, Twist. I don't know what you mean."

"Sounds like it. But you can stop it, if you want. I'm not forcing anything, least of all myself, on you. I just want it to be pure and fresh and perfect."

"Nothing is pure and fresh and perfect. You should know that. I'm allowed to have doubts, aren't I?"

"Of course."

"It is difficult. Of course it's difficult. To cheat on someone."

"You're not cheating anyone. You're being honest. That's all."

"This isn't a script, Twist. This is real."

"Real? What's real about it?"

"What's real? I'll tell you what's real. Me. My life. You can dream all you like. But then, you're not living with someone. It's easy for you."

"Easy?"

"Yes. Easy. You don't have to lie."

"I don't mind lying. In order to be honest with myself. After all, you just have to say you've gone to an exhibition. Or the mosque tea room. Or something."

"The mosque tea room?"

"Yes. No one we know ever goes there. And Flyte certainly wouldn't. Americans want to stay away from such places. They think they'll be taken hostage or something."

"Don't be stupid, Twist. You really are ridiculous sometimes. You can't take anything seriously. You think it's all a joke, don't you? You make me angry."

"Get angry then. If you want."

"Now you're behaving like a child."

"No. You are. You've had your fun. And now you've decided you've had enough. Just because it's a bit awkward."

"A bit awkward? Is that how you see it?"

"You know what I mean." I got up from the bed and walked into the bathroom. I washed my face and stepped back into the room. I sighed and looked down at Elska, so complete, so contained within her nakedness, untouchable, beyond reproach, distant, so maddeningly distant. No one could ever hope to possess such a woman.

"But you're forgetting one thing, Elska."

"What's that?"

"That we're in love."

"That's got nothing to do with it."

"Oh, yes it has. You'll have to leave him. Tell him you've had a change of heart, nothing personal, you've just come to the conclusion that there's no future to be had in it, you want to go back to Metsalump and settle down where you belong, you've had enough of dinner parties and endless conversations about the international cultural landscape. Then we can bugger off together and live by the lake. I'll become a fisherman and you can weave clothes for the twins out of reindeer tail."

"Metsalämpi."

"Metsalämpi then. Well?" I was sitting next to her, drawing rings over her breasts with my finger. I smiled. How odd it all was. You made love to a woman and then you had to seduce her afterwards.

"No. I can't."

"You can't? You can do anything you want. You're free to leave him if you wish."

"I can't." She took me by the wrist and stopped me from touching her. "No one can persuade me to do anything. Everything is so black and white with you. In love. Not in love. Free. Trapped. You trade in opposites. For you, there's no grey area."

"I don't believe in grey. Just as I don't believe in Agostini's edges. Details, just details. Details you use in art, in poetry. But you don't need them in life. No one ever has the time to look that closely."

"Who taught you that? Your father?"

"I learnt it myself. All on my own."

"It's just words."

"You've got to start somewhere."

"But the words don't really correspond to real feeling. They somehow become entirely meaningless after a while."

"Not all of them. Love is not an illusion. You love me. And I love you. Nothing can change that." I got up from the bed and poured a glass of wine from a bottle I had bought earlier. It was *la dernière goutte*. I was frustrated and angry and I threw the empty bottle into the waste-paper basket. "There you are! All used up. Empty." I proffered the glass. "Drink it!"

"I don't want it. You have it," Elska said, holding up her hand.

I lit another cigarette and looked down at her. There must have been a glow to my eyes. Why was I angry? Was not all this so inevitable? Did I really want to be with her for ever, anyway? I didn't know what was going on anymore. I'd started something and I couldn't tell what it was, other than a desire that had become increasingly destructive, to me and to Elska. Not to mention Flyte. It seemed menacing now. And I recoiled from it.

"You're wild, Twist. Too wild. You make me nervous."

This was the first time I had ever seen Elska show weakness. And the last. "You're worried you'll leave Flyte and I'll disappear into thin air. Then there'll be no one."

"There'll always be someone."

"You know, Elska, I should be telling you I've had enough. After all, I have to share you with someone."

"Share me? No one is sharing me."

"You want to have your cake and eat it."

"What does that mean?"

"Never mind. You want Flyte and you want me."

"What makes you so sure?"

"So what are you doing with me, then? Make up your mind."

"Now you're sulking."

"You say it's difficult for you and easy for me. But you're the one who sleeps with Flyte every night."

"You knew that was the set-up."

"That doesn't make it any easier."

"Perhaps we shouldn't see each other for a while."

"That's up to you."

Elska was sitting on the bed now and putting on her blouse.

She had an air of determination about her. This conversation had changed everything, already. She sighed and gave me a sidelong glance. "Flyte doesn't understand why you don't return his calls. And why you didn't come to dinner last Saturday when you never turn down our dinners."

"I gave a perfectly valid excuse."

"That you were out of town? Kajfa saw you at the Armistice the same evening on her way to the apartment. So when she told us she'd seen you, Flyte knew you were lying."

"What are we talking about here? Our love? Or a dinner party?"

"I mean, it's pretty stupid, having a drink at the Armistice when you're supposed to be out of town, isn't it?" I could tell Elska sought a pretext for a row. She had become transparent all of a sudden. Her moment of weakness had opened her up.

"What am I supposed to do? Stay in my room at the Alabama?"

"If necessary. I mean, if you're going to lie."

"How can you take the moral high ground when you're cheating on Flyte?"

"I'm not doing anything of the sort. On the contrary. I'm the one who has to lie all the time; but at least I do a good job of it."

"Well, maybe you're better at it than I am. I'm a novice. I'll learn how to do it properly. And when I'm a master, you'll never notice, you'll never know when I'm telling you the truth or not. What would you rather have for a lover? A good liar? Or a bad one?"

"Let's just not see each other for a while."

"OK."

"And call Flyte."

"I'll call him if I feel like it."

"Fine."

We stopped right there. Then we got dressed in silence and left the room behind us. At the bottom of the street, Elska turned to me.

"Good-bye."

"Good-bye, Elska."

She smiled. Then she kissed me softly on the cheek and walked away without turning back. I ran after her.

"Are you serious?"

She brushed me away. There was a tear in her eye she didn't want me to see. I think that distressed her more than the argument.

"Leave me alone."

"Well?" I said, grabbing her by the arm. "Is that it then?"

"Why do I have to decide?"

She turned away from me and walked quickly around the corner. I just stood there. It was cold. I found myself shivering. I told myself it couldn't be over. Why should it be? All couples had fights. We were no different. Were we?

31

That must have been late November or the beginning of December. I didn't call. I wasn't supposed to call Elska. So how was I supposed to call Flyte?

Any advantages to being a cad were diminishing along with the autumn light. Of course, I wasn't at all convinced Elska was serious. She had said "for a while", but that could have meant anything, just as it could have meant nothing. I thought I had begun to get to know her. But I had no idea. I wasn't going to insist on anything. That would be a waste of time; not that I didn't have time to waste.

I decided to send Flyte a card: "Dear Flyte. There's an old actor here at the Alabama called Marcello who used to look just like Peter Lorre. Or thought he did, which was enough as far as he was concerned. As for me, sorry not to have been in touch. I've been busy working on something. When I've finished, let's have a drink. And don't stop writing. Drinks are one thing, writing is another, never mix, never worry, as Dad used to say. Yours, Twist."

It was only after posting the card that I realized Flyte might think it strange of me not to have mentioned Elska. Was I becoming paranoid? Why not relax, now that the affair was probably over and done with it? We could all just forget about it and start the day fresh and clean, Bristol fashion, as if nothing had happened. A fantasy had descended briefly to reality, that was all, and now it was a memory to be reconstructed, however you wanted it reconstructed.

No. The reason I thought it was strange, or that I thought Flyte would think it strange, was because I still thought I was having an affair with Elska and, if I was having an affair with Elska, then I should have addressed the card to both of them for, in the normal world, the one in which no affair was being conducted, both of them, as a couple, were friends, were they not?

This complete uncertainty all the time only served to propel my fantasies: I was still in love, with or without her. And I still am. One day, I will awaken to find myself not in love with her. Or maybe not. Maybe I will be in love with Elska as I draw my last breath, my body will give up on me and they'll have to do something with it, stick it in a box somewhere with brass handles, but even then I probably won't stop loving her, my heart will go to Metsalumpy, just as the mammy's heart went back to Ireland to be next to Dad's within a spit of salt from that beach at Brunmore. Elska is making us all seamless reindeer-tail blankets, there's about six feet of snow over us but the neighbours are all saying it's unusually mild for the time of year. No, I won't be dead, I'll be in fine fettle, fishing mostly. We can get the other half to come over for fish and *frites*. Or maybe Agostini; there must be a lot of edges to look at on summer nights, at least enough to stop him from being bored if he can't find a girl to talk to.

The twins won't be permitted to follow in the footsteps because there won't be any. They won't need to become actors or poets or anything else, no need to trouble them with all that inside thinking, they can do something sensible, nothing if they want to, learn how to make summerhouses out of timber or fridges out of snow or perhaps become prize-winning fishermen of Finland, get the Nobel Prize for Fishery.

Yes, we'll have twins, even though twins are supposed to skip a generation, rules were made to be broken and this is one that is heading for a breakage, the mammy's mammy was a twin, and Dad's uncle, for that matter. Our twins, even if they're not twins, will definitely have twins, even taking into account the skipping of the generations, for if they really are twins then, normally, their grandchildren or grand-nephews or grand-nieces should be twins. The best way to think of it is that there will definitely be twins on the horizon somewhere. I haven't mentioned this to Elska, because I understand that for a woman having a child is like trying to get a grand piano through a keyhole, and I don't think it's fair to set Elska thinking about two grand pianos in one go, as it were. Not fair at all.

The other half and me had it easy because of our twin-ship. No doubt about it. No infant is going to attack you when you've got four fists, when you've got someone riding shotgun for you on a permanent basis. Yes, it's so easy, so easy, being a twin. With the telepathy, as well. Easy. Pain is a great conductor and if things are not going brilliantly and one of us falls off a ladder raised to an impossible dream, the other half is always there to catch him. That's what the mountaineer said. "I'm not afraid of falling, it's the landing that bothers me."

Had a point.

32

I'm sure I'm not the only chap who is dreaming of Elska. There's probably a whole army of them out there, marching up and down and all over the place with their kitbags stuffed full with Elska fantasies. But I've got the best one, the most real one, for did Elska not say that Metsalumpy was where she wanted to be? I very much doubt she tells them all about Metsalumpy. That would be cheating, you just can't do that sort of thing, tell everyone about Metsalumpy. If she did, the place would be so crowded there'd be nowhere to hang your hat, let alone drop your kitbag onto the floor. Besides, fantasies are the most precious thing of all, they're like really good poems, there's no point in talking about them until they've happened, otherwise they won't be any good anymore.

So: it was December, according to the noughts, the noughts of three hundred, which are still there even though the train has slowed to a third of that speed. Yes, I can still use them, the *jumelles*, the binoculars in the feminine, to check dates and such-like. They work well, they were made for long journeys.

I was alone. But not alone. I'm never alone in Paris, unless I want to be. I was just giving Flyte and Elska the slip until I saw what to do and how to be. Agostini had been travelling. Quite often, he goes away for months at a time. And then I run into him, at the market bar, or in the Rally. If he's not in town, I always think of him in some impossibly exotic location, taking pictures of pretty girls in frocks, Rajasthan perhaps? A neat shot of rectangles, dyed material in primary colours at the feet of a thin and towering beauty as she skips over the dust and sand, Agostini screaming for stillness or for motion, for the world to stop turning for a moment so he can get it all in the frame correctly.

"Hello, Agostini."

"Hello, Twist."

"So?"

"Been away. Los Angeles. Japan. Bali."

"Any good?"

"Yes. It's got nothing to do with the rag trade. It's just pretty girls to me. And what's wrong with that?"

"Nothing, Agostini. I didn't say there was."

"Those models get a complex though. They think they have to be educated. But you don't have to be educated if you're just drop-dead beautiful, do you? You just have to know how to do the right things, like look great and one day bring up children and cook pasta."

"That's right, Agostini."

"America's had it, though. I used to like it. But not now. The Americans have lost their sense of humour. They don't eat properly, they don't drink anymore. I'm not sure whether they even have sex. Their women are scary. You can't flirt with them anymore. They sue you for *harcèlement*."

"Harassment, Agostini. Harassment."

"Whatever you want to call it. I don't even know what it is. If you're not allowed to flirt with women, what's going to happen? They'll stop being beautiful because they won't need to be. There'll be no point. All the women will become ugly, they'll change their minds, because that's what women do, but then no one will be interested in them, they'll just be stuck in offices working for businessmen and they won't even be allowed to smoke. Nature works like that. After all, we used to have tails and then we didn't need them anymore."

"Maybe the whole place'll die off," I suggested. "There must be some Red Indians or some Irish-Indians left and I bet they still know how to have a good time. They can start up again, fishing and breeding. All the American-Americans will grow old and there'll be no one to replace them but the Indians will all be fucking away to their hearts' content."

"That would be better. I don't really mind, though. What difference does it all make, Twist? Paris is what matters and here you can do what you like. Even ugly women look great in Paris. I saw a woman cop the other day and she was actually quite sexy. I asked her out for a drink. I mean, why not? Know what I mean, Twist?"

"I know what you mean, Agostini."

"Yeah, I said you can bring your gun if you like and we'll go dancing or something."

"Sounds fun, Agostini."

"Don't tell Flyte, Twist. About what I said. You know, about Americans. I don't want him to get the wrong idea. I like Flyte. How is he, by the way?"

"I haven't seen him for a while."

"Still with Elska?"

"What do you mean?"

"I mean is he still with Elska?"

"Why shouldn't he be?"

"No reason."

"Agostini, tell me the truth. Do you think there's any reason why they shouldn't be together all of a sudden?"

"No. I said no, didn't I?"

"Then why did you ask?"

"Well, I got the impression they weren't very happy all of a sudden. When I saw them last."

"When was that?"

"Oh, ages ago. Beginning of September. I was at one of their dinners. The Spanish girl was there. You remember the Spanish girl? They didn't seem to be talking to each other very much."

"Maybe it was a phase. Couples often have phases, don't they?"

"Yeah. A phase."

33

I remember one day awakening with a nasty hangover. I lay in the half-light of my room and the pain that ran through my head went straight to my heart as I remembered Elska, in all her sad beauty, for her beauty had become edged with teeth all of a sudden. I wanted to hold her, badly. The telephone rang. It was Agostini.

"No plans, Agostini. I haven't thought about today."

"It's Christmas."

"Is it?"

We went for a walk. Later, we had dinner at La Coupole with the old ladies seated on their own, at tables around us. I was so in love with Elska that day. I had no idea where she was but I imagined her somewhere, with Flyte, laughing, opening up a present that was probably a necklace or a ring.

What was I to do? I couldn't even talk to Agostini about it. I was lovesick. And I'd never been lovesick before. Not like that.

"You're sad, Twist. Don't be sad," Agostini said.

"Can't help it. I hate Christmas."

"Just forget it's Christmas. Pretend it's something else. You're an actor."

So, I forgot about it, I forgot about Christmas and Elska and I had a drink with Agostini instead. Late in the night, after we had parted, I went back to the Alabama; Wolf was there, as usual, at reception.

"You missed her," he said.

"Who?"

"A beautiful woman, Seamus. I've never seen her before."

"What did she look like?"

"I told you. A beauty. Black hair and blue eyes."

"Elska."

"She left something for you."

Wolf handed me a small parcel and I went up to the room. I stepped out onto the balcony and looked out to Paris. The sky was quite clear, there was a sliver of moon and some stars sparkling. I inhaled it all and I knew that life was good and that it was meant to be lived, not just looked at from afar. I knew I was sad for all that was lost, even though I was just as convinced that anything I wanted was waiting for me, out there, within the winter night. Everything that existed was meant to be. And all that was absent was of equal note.

I went back into my room and opened the parcel. It was an empty book, a leather-bound volume for writing. "Happy Christmas, Twist, Love Elska," it said inside.

That's the book in front of me now. I'm filling it faster than I imagined. It's been easy. But not too easy. Difficult. But not too difficult. And the only reason I'm doing it is because when I packed my stuff this morning, I found it in a drawer. It fell into my lap, as it were. Well, I thought to myself. Might as well use it. Otherwise it'll go to waste, won't it?

Part Six
TRIPERIE

34

I look up. The girl has come back. And we've stopped all of a sudden. Right here, in the tunnel. Yes, the train has stopped and we are stuck in this monstrous construction, destruction, a great big hole miles away from anything. It's preposterous! I'm sitting opposite a strange girl under the sea, lighting a cigarette for her, when I should be writing everything down in the book Elska gave me for writing. And I'm going to be late, the other half will get to the tankard before me, Sandra will greet him and ask him when I'm coming, and he'll say I've arrived but I won't have done, because the speed didn't just go from maximum to minimum, it went from maximum to nothing. To zero.

"We've stopped," I declare. For some reason, I think the girl will tell me why.

"Yes," she answers, turning from the window, which is supposed to be my window, towards me.

"I have to go back to the other carriage now."

"I think your boyfriend is a little upset with you."

"He's not my boyfriend."

"So. You don't have a boyfriend?"

"No. I met him last night in a club. He invited me to London. I've never been before. I haven't got anything with me because I didn't go home. I don't have any money and I only have one cigarette left. I have hardly spoken to him. And I can't remember what his name is. All I know is that he doesn't smoke. I'm not even sure I like him."

"Jesus, I thought I was disorganised. Ask to look at his passport photograph because you've got a thing about passport photographs. Then you'll find out what his name is. I'll give you a packet of cigarettes. And some money, if you want. If I can find some. I'm a bit short but there are a lot of pockets in a three-piece suit. If you can't be bothered with the passport, think up a nickname for him. That's what we used to do."

"Nickname?"

"Yes. *Sobriquet.* You know what I mean. Lofty. Or Shorty. I don't know. Grumpy."

"Grumpy?"

"Yeah, one of *les sept nains. Blanche Neige* and all that."

I offer her a Martell miniature. She takes it.

"So. What's your name?"

"Isabelle. And you?"

"Twist."

"Twist? Is that a surname?"

"It's a nickname. But usually we call ourselves by our surnames."

"We?"

"Uprights. Moraes. Flyte. Braine. Agostini. But not Marcello, who is also an upright. Don't ask me why. I can't really explain it. The thing is, there is no hard and fast rule. We want to avoid that."

"I don't understand."

"Don't worry. There's nothing to understand."

"Are you writing a book?"

"No. I'm just writing. I've never written before and now I'm doing it. Or trying to. I don't know whether it's supposed to be easy or difficult. Dad said you should always be careful when it was easy but not half as careful as when it was difficult. He knew how to do it. Perhaps it's one of those things that's easy to do but not easy to do well, or easy to do well as long as you are already good at it. The most important thing is to make it *look* easy."

"I don't quite understand what you are saying."

"No one does. It's an enigma. Like this tunnel we're in. Stuck in."

"Why?"

"Well, they built it, they had this idea, they worked it all out. And the two ends met perfectly. That's the enigma. But then, they probably used computers, didn't they?"

"So, what is it you are writing? Is it a story?"

"I think so."

"It's a book already. All those pages. I couldn't do that."

"It's supposed to be linear. But now the train has stopped. And I've started talking to you."

"I'm sorry."

"Don't apologise. That's how it's supposed to be. Besides, you're a nice girl and we're stuck in a tunnel."

"I think it's a book. You should get it published."

"No. That's not important. I'm writing it for myself. And when it's done, I won't ever need to read it."

"Others might."

"Others? And who might they be? No. I'll probably just give it to someone."

"Who?"

"Elska."

"Who's Elska?"

"I'm not telling you." I give her a cigarette and light it for her. "You look a bit pale."

"I think it's a hangover."

"Like a line of cocaine?"

35

January in Paris, puddles catching reflections, grim and leaden, half a leg here, stiletto heel there, cops in overcoats helping infants across the street, shoal after shoal rushing down the boulevard heading for open water, empty restaurants, cold snap from the north, everyone scurrying up the stairs with work in their hands, awaiting winter's end. How many Januarys have I passed within the Paris orbit, always the same, or practically so? There's something about always knowing what you're in for. When we were small-sized, Dad would take us to school and then lose his morning in the Rally, scribbling or gassing or drinking, or some infernal variant of all three.

"Well, boys. Keep a weather eye on each other. Pay attention. Try and learn something. Might come in useful later on down the road."

A month passed and I languished in the Alabama, chatting to Marcello in the corridor or lying in my room, reading. I reread *The Good Soldier* and, thinking of Flyte, *The Great Gatsby*, in which Fitzgerald says that "*life is best viewed from a single window*". And I read for the first time *The Alexandria Quartet*; I think Lawrence Durrell had Irish blood in him somewhere. Can't see a proper Englishman writing that kind of a book. "*It is not love that is blind, but jealousy*," he says, at one point, or has the narrator say it.

I thought about that. Was I jealous of Flyte? Strangely not. There was a fairness to it all, a sort of playground fairness of the "you found it first" ilk. So how could I be? I thought of them going to bed together, to test myself, but I couldn't get further than Flyte folding up his Brooks Brothers boxer shorts. Just couldn't picture him. Picture it.

If I awoke in the night, or couldn't sleep, or came back to the hotel late, I might listen to Wolf or Régis in reception. They are like my brothers, we understand each other, so sometimes nothing would be said. I'd find a bottle somewhere and we would drink in silence. Or listen to what visitors might ask as they made their enquiries. "Do you have a non-smoking room?" asked one.

"No one is obliging you to smoke, sir."

Occasionally, I went out with Agostini and we talked about women, or girls, or anything that came to mind, countless dialogues hardly worthy of the limited space now available in this book for writing. One night, he turned to me:

"What happened to that woman?"

"Which woman?"

"The woman you were with? Who was with someone?"

"Nothing. Nothing much."

"Shouldn't try to steal someone else's woman, Twist. Unless you are very serious about it. Because it's a serious business. Someone tried to steal Aunt Maria and Uncle Guiseppe cut his balls off."

I walked home and went straight to my room. I started going through my belongings and I came across the Magnum. I'd forgotten to give it back after doing that silly gangster film. I walked out onto the balcony and held it up to the moon. I imagined I was far away, in Mad Joe's garden, or on some patch of tundra on the outskirts of Metsalumpy, and I took aim and fired the beast. The recoil smashed my elbow into the window pane and broke the glass as the dummy round went off, a message from me to the gods to hear some unspoken prayer. They must have been asleep, not even the report of the Magnum would have awoken them; it did awaken my neighbours though, a party of Germans, who were soon standing outside my door in paisley dressing gowns.

"Don't worry. It's only a gun."

I lay on the bed, thinking of life and death and love and the balls of the man who had tried to steal Agostini's Aunt Maria and I tried to shy away from the seriousness of what I – what we, me and Elska – had done. And then I knew I could never avoid it, it was ineluctable, as serious as anything could be. I was in love with her. And that was all there was to it.

36

After pondering Fitzgerald's beautiful story, I found I had transformed Flyte into that peculiar mythomaniac, Gatsby, and I half expected him to end up face down in a swimming pool somewhere, shot by a *garagiste*.

Of course, Flyte was not really like Gatsby at all; no one could be. He was more like the other chap, Daisy's husband, Tom Buchanan; but, had he lived in another age, that age, I could have imagined him sauntering out onto a massive lawn on Long Island, making arrangements for a party and showing off his shirt collection to a Daisy lookalike. The fact is I never understood Flyte, neither then nor now. He was actually full of surprises. He betrayed Elska. And what man in their right mind would do that?

Marcello was getting older too quickly. He wanted to talk to me all the time. He must have known he didn't have long. He would get me into his room and there would be a brass cup waiting to be filled with whisky and a plate of nuts beside it, on a low table. He would show me things – a poster for a show from the Thirties, a funny hat, a notice from a paper so old it felt brittle to the touch – or he would just lie down on his bed, talking to me of the past.

"When I was young, Seamus, I could do anything I wished, without so much as a second thought. I saw in nothing, everything, the whole world; I could tell what was going on on the other side, I could see through walls, survey the passage of the stars, I was immortal and, of course, a genius. And now? I have to think first, I wait and I think, for I know that, as long as I am patient, something will always happen. Remember that, Twist, something always happens."

Along the confused tangents which constituted his memory, addled with all the dope they gave him, Marcello sought, within the past, the beginnings of stories, reinventing them and guiding them forwards by the power of his imagination. People and places appeared to him as if on a stage, gaudy backdrops lifted and changed as characters came and went, some real, some imagined, all smiling at him, paying their respects as the old impersonator made his way through the last act of his life. I loved Marcello and I always will love him, he was a dad to me and Dad's best friend and an uncle and many other things and the fact that he is dead changes nothing, for one can miss the dead badly but still talk and listen to them now and then. Death is just a curtain, faded, a little rotten, transparent in patches, and not the wall the cemetery would have you believe it is. No one's putting me in a cemetery, they can throw my ashes into the wandering foam or sprinkle them over the garden in Metsalumpy, but not in a box beyond a wall, face up to nothing.

Another time, Marcello spoke of a girl: "You remember the make-up girl I told you about, when I was being filmed that time? I called her Tini Pond and we became lovers. She had stars in her eyes and the biggest eyelashes I ever saw. When we made love, she never looked at me, but I could see those eyelashes framed against the ceiling, a shadow which still flickers in my mind, a fan designed to cool my ardour. I told her I loved her and she said it was a kind thing to say. Imagine! A kind thing! I'm not sure whether I did love her then. But I love her now and I cannot tell her. She is gone.

"For a while, Tini Pond was always at my side. She did my make-up and was soon appearing in the act, helping me with the Flaming Bath Trick. I insisted she wore a tutu. She would handcuff me, then tie me with a rope, making sure my ankles were securely fastened, that my arms were tied close to my body and the noose around my neck was clearly visible to the audience. She would pour petrol into a bath of water set just beside me in the middle of the stage and I would fall into it. Then she would throw a match into the bath and smile broadly at the audience, jettisoning the dead match with a flourish, opening her arms in a gesture of miraculous absurdity as the flames reached up behind her and the smoke engulfed the stage.

"This I had taught her to do during many rehearsals. 'You've just set me on fire, Tini.' I would tell her. 'It's a big moment. Transmit that moment to the people. I know you can do it. And I want you to make a big effort. After all, I will have my own work cut out for me in the bath.'

"The first time we tried it, I jumped into the bath and waited for the petrol to catch fire, while Tini Pond struggled to find a book of matches I had given her. I nearly drowned.

"The second time, Tini Pond found the book of matches, but they were soaking wet. As she tried another match, then another, the stage manager stood in the wings, doubtless thinking we had developed a new angle on the trick by postponing the lighting of the bath to heighten the tension. He was wrong. I nearly drowned once again. The stage manager finally intervened by pushing Tini Pond to one side and throwing his Zippo lighter into the bath, so that, when I finally emerged, both he and Tini Pond were standing in front of me, their arms outstretched, beaming at the audience. Nobody could see me. Half unconscious, I tripped on the lip of the bath and fell between them. They picked me up like a dead weight. The audience thought it was all done on purpose as a joke.

"The third and last time, Tini Pond managed to light the bath but was standing too close to it, so that her tutu caught fire. When I appeared, I was also on fire. Tini Pond was supposed to douse me with a blanket in case of any emergency, but, as she was on fire, that was impossible. The stage manager had to put us out with a fire extinguisher and we both ended up in hospital with second-degree burns.

"That was the last of the Flaming Bath Trick. And the last of Tini Pond. I never saw her again. My last memory of her is of her singed eyelashes, blinking an apology to me. She was a beauty, Twist. And she nearly killed me. She is with me now, she has been sent to help me perform the next act. I just hope she does a better job this time."

37

I was walking through the Gardens one day when I realized it was spring. The winter appeared to me as one long, sleepless night, and I rejoiced, like a prisoner on early release.

When I returned to the Alabama, there was a message for me. From Flyte. I called him back immediately. He asked me to come over to the apartment. I suggested neutral ground, as tactfully as I could. But he insisted. Elska would be out, apparently. So I went round that evening, after dinner.

Should I confess? Look, Flyte. I had an affair with Elska. It just happened. But it's over now.

It was getting warmer but Flyte had made a fire. He was holding a poker in his hand when he opened the door for me and I suddenly imagined him hitting me over the head with it. "We hardly see each other these days, Twist. Why is that?"

"I've been busy."

He put the poker in the grate, went off to wash his hands and then led me into his study.

"So, what have you been up to?" he said perkily, handing me a drink.

"Bit of this, bit of that. Reading books. Listening to Marcello. Listening to Agostini. Going through some papers of Dad's. You know, that biographer got much more wrong than I gave him credit for. He should have been a novelist. People think they can recreate someone's life simply by recording a series of events. But events hide more than they reveal. Dad was an enigma. Impossible to describe. But, if you're going to try, better to concentrate on what the poems, rather than the neighbours, have to say. No one ever understands another person, even if they spend a lifetime together. Still, you can't blame the chap for trying. Got to make a living, like everyone else, so why not do it out of the dead?"

"Quite so, Twist. Why don't you do it?"

"What?"

"Write the biography of your father."

"I can't write, Flyte. Can't act. Can't write. But there's no harm in that. I'm going to catch a tuna the size of a bus and it won't have headlamps for eyes, it'll have dustbin lids. We'll be eating off it from now to eternity."

"Who's we? Got yourself a girlfriend?"

"All of us, Flyte. All of us."

"Speaking of which, you should come for dinner. We like having you."

He seemed decidedly melancholic that evening, resigned rather than tired. I asked him what the matter was.

"I don't know quite what I'm doing anymore."

"I told you to write."

"That's not it. I am writing."

"Good. Don't waste your time with anything else. It's not worth it."

"Sometimes, I feel like going back to New York. You know how it is."

"Home? Is that it? Can you manage that?"

"You manage it."

"I'm not sure where home is exactly. Perhaps that's why. Not that I really manage anything. But I thought you didn't like New York."

"It's not so much a question of liking. It's more to do with feeling my time is up in Paris and I need the change," he said, taking a swig of bourbon.

"New York's great. If you're fit and that's what you're in the mood for. Got to be in the mood for it, though. It'll eat you up for breakfast otherwise and spit you out. What about Elska?"

"She doesn't mind. Either way. She has some friends in New York. She likes it."

"I can't imagine Elska being ambivalent about such a thing. I mean, it's not like deciding which restaurant to go to." I felt myself siding with her and made an effort to pull back the camera a little. "But you know what she wants, I imagine. How is she, anyway?"

"She's well."

"What's she doing these days?"

"Elska doesn't do much. Doesn't feel she has to. Or need to, for that matter." Flyte got up from his chair and poured fresh drinks from a tray on the sideboard.

"So, I'm actually going to New York next week, to meet some editors and see how I feel about it all. I want to go on my own to check it out. Elska is staying here. I'll be away for ten days."

"Everything's all right between you, isn't it? I mean, there isn't a problem or anything?" My suspicions had been raised and I could see a crystal glimmer of hope shine through the tumbler Flyte handed me. Hope and sympathy, a curious mixture of opposites, for my attitude towards Flyte had not really changed at all, despite all that had happened, despite my deceit. This sympathy almost made me tell him: it was a feeling controlled, above all, by the need to be honest. I saw him suffering, I blamed myself, I found myself acting simply as a friend all of a sudden, rather than a friend and a cad. I suspected they were having problems and naturally assumed it was my fault, a curious blend of vanity and guilt, I must say, but almost palpable nonetheless. Deceit always upsets the balance, belittling certain feelings, emphasizing others, yet once it is removed, everything is restored to a former glory of all the finest attributes. Whatever was going on inside my head, in my heart I knew that, if I was ever going to admit it, then now was the only time. Afterwards, I would be deemed even worse a criminal for not having done so and for having deliberately played with the situation, above all for having manipulated it for my benefit.

I was as confused as anyone can ever be. I didn't even know whether or not I was still having an affair with Elska. Everything was so inconclusive. I hadn't seen her for months. We had just had a quarrel, that was all. I had no idea how things were or could be. She had felt too much pressure, too much insecurity. I could hardly blame her for that, it was normal, but it was hardly sufficient to destroy whatever we had going together. Or was it?

I can see Flyte now, as we sit stuck in this infernal hole, back at his desk, looking at me carefully as he brought his glass to his lips and sipped his beloved bourbon. What a moment of emptiness that was, that silence which hid my doubts as I considered whether or not to tell him the truth. An air of complete abstraction overcame his features as he put the glass down and took a cigarette from a silver case and also, startlingly, a clear nervousness, for his hand trembled slightly as he lit it. Why was he nervous? What truth was he hiding?

"Problem? Not at all. Everything's fine."

"You're not still worried, then? About what she's thinking?"

"No. That passed. It was difficult for a while. Much better now."

"Good. She loves you, Flyte."

"Does she? Does she really?"

"Of course!"

"She's a great woman." He nodded to himself. I smiled.

And he smiled back at me, through the cigarette smoke. "You know, Twist, I'll have to ask you another favour."

"What's that?"

"Well, keep an eye on her while I'm away. We don't have many real friends. I know you're busy, but she's very fond of you. Take her out or something."

"Sure," I answered, casually.

"You're one of the very few people I can actually trust."

38

I called Elska the day Flyte left, but she was out. I left a message. "Hello, Elska. It's Twist. How are you? What's happening? Call me."

I didn't expect her to call me back, but she did, the next morning.

"Hello." She sounded as if she were calling from Metsalumpy.

"Do you want to meet?"

"I don't know."

"What does that mean?"

"It means I don't know."

"Well, I know," I said. Nearly four months had passed, but all those days and nights vanished in the time it took for her to laugh down the telephone.

"You do, do you?"

"Sure. It's lunchtime."

We met in the brasserie where we had had our first lunch. We kissed each other on the cheek, like friends, and during the meal we conversed like strangers. There was an interesting show up. Painting. Some good movies playing. And someone had brought out a novel that wasn't quite as good as his last one. I can act. So can Elska, her whole being is an act, the most beautiful I ever saw. But this wasn't acting. This was faking it.

"Enough of all this, Elska. We're being ridiculous. Let's get out of here. We're going on a trip. To the sea."

"What are you talking about?"

"I've got a car outside. I rented it."

"You're crazy, Twist."

"Someone's got to be. Otherwise we'll be stuck here for ever talking about books and films and paintings."

"I'll have to pack."

"You don't need to pack."

We finished our lunch in silence. After a while I said, "What do you need to pack for?" and Elska laughed. That was it. I paid the bill, we got in the car and drove away, through Paris, along the *quai* and out. The sky cleared in the west so that is where we headed, where the sun was already low in the sky. We got onto the *autoroute* and accelerated, the journey took on a life of its own and we became simple players in it, subject to its own momentum. Stuck in the tunnel now, I can feel that car charging along the road impatiently, me and Elska sitting in it as if it were the first and last journey we would ever take.

"I haven't seen any Metsalumpy signs yet," I said.

"What are we doing?"

"We're heading for the wandering foam." I turned to her. "Well, Flyte did tell me to look after you."

"Don't make jokes about it. It's not funny."

"What's not funny about it?"

Elska laughed. And I laughed too. And all the deceit which had initially bound us returned to bless and to damn us as we drove, for it was deceit as much as love, from the beginning to the end, for all of us, not just Elska and me, but Flyte and the rest of the world, for that matter, a world I now see, not through the single window but through the windscreen of an anonymous, rented car. Wiped of a cloudburst, it transports us at chosen speed through time, from the promise of a first kiss to the promise of another, and still another, in a room by the sea, far away, all of them stolen, like time, every one.

The sun set as we journeyed in silence and it was late by the time we reached the coast. We found a room in a hotel by the beach and we ate oysters in a nearby restaurant. We were no longer friends, or strangers, but fellow conspirators in some endless crime.

"No," said Elska. "I don't want to talk about love. Ever again. I don't want to talk about anything anymore. I'm just following an instinct, an instinct which is my instinct but which so often feels strange to me, as if it were not me at all but a guiding hand from some former, treacherous life. And this hand terrifies me even as it promises me pleasure."

"Instinct can be scary. No one ever denied it that."

"You are brute instinct, Twist. You never think. You think you think. But you don't. You're acting. All the time. Yes, you frighten me sometimes, even more than my own instinct. Is that why I find you hard to resist?"

"Well, it can't be my manners." I raised my glass and smiled. Elska was not amused. "I can't really imagine you being frightened of anything," I added, setting my glass back on the table.

"Can't you? That just proves how little you know me. You think you do. But it's just another illusion."

"I never said that. I never claimed I knew you."

"You just look at me. You like what you see, even if you don't get what you planned on. It's mostly a game for you."

"Then you don't know me either. I know you as much as I want to know you. I'm not fooling myself. I never said I had all the answers."

"I suppose we're using each other."

"Elska! I thought you said you didn't want to talk about it!"

"I'm sorry. But it's true, isn't it? Love is just a means of manipulation. It's terrible sometimes."

"Everything's terrible sometimes. Being alone is terrible sometimes."

"And, when one person has had enough of it, no longer needs it, then it's over. I suppose I'm guilty of that."

"No one's guilty. And nothing is so simple. Surely?"

"Perhaps. But there is that side to it, isn't there? In the end, all we're trying to do is to protect ourselves, buying security, selling our souls. The whole thing is a deception, from start to finish. Whichever way you look at it. Everyone's using each other. It's disgusting."

"Nonsense. I don't know what, or who, you're talking about."

"Not disgusting. Human. Pitifully human. Weak."

"Nothing wrong with being weak, is there? Why do people have to pretend to be something when they're not? We're all weak. We can be strong. But it's always an effort. The natural state is vulnerable, insecure; yes, weak. Now finish your oysters and shut up!"

Another laugh and she relaxed. I couldn't tell whether she was talking about me or Flyte; or, rather, I felt she could have said exactly the same thing to either of us. She was talking in generalities and I wasn't buying it. She'd been thinking too much. I'd been thinking too much as well. But I hadn't come to any conclusions. That was the difference.

We went back to the hotel and fell into each other's arms and we didn't talk anymore because there wasn't any need. And nothing we would have said would have meant anything. All was resolved within that embrace, and all forgotten. The best way to cheat time is to either forget about it or lose yourself in someone else's body.

"I love you, Elska," I said, in the darkness. And she said nothing. Nothing at all, she just lay in my arms and fell asleep. Then, as now, I could not have imagined how she felt about me.

If I were to be really honest with myself, I would say I didn't actually care. My view of it all, of the affair that is, is entirely conditioned by the impossible love I created for Elska from the start. I thought that if I kept it like that I would be able to control it.

How vain is that?

39

The next day, we took the ferry to an island. I can't remember what the island was called, but all islands are the same, Conrad's mountain-tops, small worlds smelling of the sea. The sea, the ceaseless rasp and roar, me and the other half and Myles gripped by the waves and breakers, our shrill voices rising through the spray, the other half on one side of the mammy, me on the other, Myles jumping into a great bucket of wave and onto an errant urchin. The wet and wavy sea. Running over the sand to a boarding house with a bag of mackerel and not letting anyone have them, keeping them in our room away from the grown-ups.

"They're ours, those fish, we caught 'em and no one's eating 'em!"

"Come on, boys, don't be ridiculous. Hand them over!"

Elska and I stood on that ship, starboard side, while the wind came up strong from the north-west and the sea rolled as we headed south. There was a swell and the ship fell through the troughs, bringing the spray right up to our noses. I put my arm around Elska, protecting her, and it is this image which comes to me, and this alone, whenever I first think of her; it was this which began the book for writing and will finish the book for writing, to the accompaniment of my poem for the other half, still a surprise, just as long as we stop being stuck and start moving from deep under the waves. This book which might also be a letter to you, Elska, as long as you forgive me for the bad bits, wherever they happen to be.

It was a short passage, but a fine one at that: there were few other passengers, the ship was near empty, the sky was blue, the sea the darkest and most slippery ever. There was a magic to it straight out of Marcello's hat, as if Paris had been churned up by the screws and left bubbling in the foam behind us, along with all the sleepless nights and shrinking dreams of winter, the natural flotsam of a crowded life and the jetsam which is its detritus, all washed away by that big, heaving sea. The sea makes me believe that existence can be blessed with a purity, unhindered, perfect almost; and a ship, however battered and bullied, however ailing, seems the only truly poetic object in a world of objects so clumsily pressed for need. The sky looks over us and God may find comfort in those who look back at all that is wrong, contrite, even if just for a moment.

Elska and I could finally forget the past, forget the future, reinventing ourselves for the benefit of the camera, and the love that had teased us and brought us so much sadness now brought a flush to her cheeks:

"Immortalise us, stranger! Don't worry about the edges!"

Where is that stranger now, that immortalising stranger? He swayed on deck and grasped the rail and we laughed at his misfortune, but kindly so, for he laughed back at us as he held the little yellow box in his hand and snapped the picture. He was like us, trying as best he could to freeze the image, to capture and to hold it. Arm in arm before that bright sky, we were, for the length of that shutter speed at least, entirely innocent, like children almost. So, where is the stranger now? Does he remember us? Can he now kindly step forwards and prove for us that we were perfectly, sublimely happy then and that it was manifestly clear we belonged to each other? Belong to each other? As much as any two people can belong to each other?

The island had little and all we needed. There was a hotel. We ate fish for dinner and went to bed. Our sex had a pattern to it; it had become a premeditation, the sure-fired anticipation of expectancy, as good as anything might possibly promise to be, better than good, as good as it gets. It was more of a poem than a picture, even if the act itself is usually best left undescribed. Everything is approximate, except the touch of skin.

"I know what will happen," I said, as we returned to the mainland.

"No one knows."

"You will go back to Flyte and I will sit in the Alabama wondering whether we should see each other again. And then one day we will say good-bye and I will take a train to drink Guinness with the other half. But I won't meet a girl anymore."

"Yes, you will."

"It's funny, we never really started anything. And, when we did, all we did was try to stop it. That must be love of some sort, even if it's a strange sort."

"I don't know, Twist."

"You always say that. Then you say you do know. Just like you say you don't want to talk about it. Then you talk about it. Do you always do the opposite of what you say?"

"No."

Part Seven

BOUCHERIE
TRIPERIE

40

I am not there. There is no island, no foam. And there is no window seat. The book for writing lies open, the train is stopped still and the memory is lost within the terrible darkness of the tunnel, the ultimate absence noted, a foretaste of London, City of Crime. The girl is with me, I have used a script-full of platitudes to charm her, the man who is larger than nature intended but who doesn't seem to have a name is in No Smoking, and I have brought the two of us to this absurd *cul-de-sac* in order to exact my revenge on Elska, to betray her, to assuage my guilt and longing.

I knew if I could get her into the heads, I'd be ahead of the game. I broke off from my row with Elska, in the restaurant by the sea, when Elska says, "It's mostly a game to you," or perhaps a bit later, in the night, when she left me wondering, wandering, to provide the girl with a line of cocaine from a small fold Agostini gave me last night. I don't use the stuff, but Agostini said it would help the hangover for the trip to the other half and slipped it into my top pocket.

"It's also a good way to pick up girls, Twist," he added, authoritatively.

I had to get rid of it somehow, didn't I? And now I'm cutting up a line by the sink with an expired telephone card, I can't quite believe it, but seeing is believing and I catch our reflection in the hall of mirrors that makes of this place the ultimate absurdity: a lavatory below the flushing sea. This girl is a good-time girl and that's what she wants, so I'm offering it to her. Neither of us has a bank-note to snort it up because we're both broke, so I take the edge off my train ticket folder and turn it round my pencil.

And now the game is ahead of me. I am holding her, kissing her, grasping and pawing at her sweater which must be made of something elastic, I'm putting my hands under her shirt and feeling her tuppenny breasts, lowering my face to them and circling her nipples with a tongue still tingling with cocaine, the hands now move down to her skirt and I raise her up onto the wash-basin, I'm searching in my pockets for the condoms I never use, damn their backwards- and forwardness, I'm taking the condom out of the packet and the girl is looking at me as if I'm about to do a magic act not even Marcello could have performed without laughing, I've got the thing in my hand and I'm trying to get it onto my prick and all the time I know I should be writing in the book made for writing, to finish the story about me and Elska and Flyte, all of a sudden, which is a pretty funny expression when you think of it, the train lurches forward and I fall between the girl's thighs, I'm inside the girl, inside the heads, inside a train, inside a tunnel, inside a world which has begun moving again, just as I'm moving inside the girl who speaks excellent English and hasn't brought anything with her because she didn't get a chance to go home and pack, who doesn't have a penny with her, or a cigarette for that matter, nor anything else, except a drunken and forlorn Irish former actor moving about inside her, like a finger seeking a switch in the darkness.

"You surprise me," she says, as I slip out of her.

"I surprise me."

"We're moving again."

"Yes. We're moving. I'm going to be late for lunch. And I have a book to finish."

"So it is a book, after all."

"Who can say?"

"You're crazy."

"That's what Elska always says."

"Who's Elska?"

"I'm not telling."

41

The girl is gone. I might have dreamed it. I search through my pockets. Seven condoms. No. I didn't dream it.

Never thought I would, either. It's like swimming with your gumboots on. What a sorry business compared to the inside of Elska! I thought if I did that, if I betrayed Elska and her memory, it would change things. It didn't. All I did was use the girl and now I feel shame and rot seeping through the entire corpus. I am crazy. Aren't I? I also did a line for myself, it doesn't suit me and I don't like it, I was just doing it to be a good host, as it were, and now my pulse is racing faster than the damned train, not that the train is going fast, it's shaking rather than rattling, even though it's picked up speed a little as we near the exit of the tunnel.

Yes, soon we'll be out of this thing, this hole, and into the light of England, if they've got any; soft England, satanic mills, Pudding Island, all greens everywhere with lots of grey areas, cricket, damp lawns and fish hanging from the ceiling of Waterloo Station. The other half says it's all modern now, which is a pity. Why is modern good? They never called Dad modern. And he was good. They'll be reading his stuff long after they've got bored with being modern. Or post-modern. What the hell is post-modern? It's just words but the wrong words, because you can have the right words and put them in the right place if you set your mind to it. If you think about it, which Elska says I never do.

The only thing is I am going to be late for the lunch with the other half. He'll understand. The party will have to start without me, but it will still be *exactly* as I imagined it, it has to be. It just needs slight modification, that's all. Sandra will take care of him for the half-hour we've missed. Sandra knew us all and she will speak of Dad and of all the lunches. For Sandra, lunch is a clock and all time is counted in fish; she knew the mammy when they were infants which is why we used to go there, so there will be a lot of fish to catch up on when the other half appears.

I am looking through the window again. There is a sucking, swishing sound, a massive breath of displaced air as the train finally exits the tunnel of love and darkness and we are now carried off into England. England! We're chugging along nice and sedately now, as if we were in a fairground, which is a not a bad way to describe the place. I always liked fairgrounds, but not as much as I liked the circus.

Why wasn't I brave enough to just go ahead and become a tiger-tamer? That's what I should have told Holy God when he asked me what I was going to be. Maybe that would have been the one thing he wouldn't have laughed at.

"What do you think of that, boys? Seamus is going to be a tiger-tamer!"

The whole pub in Ireland would have raised itself to shaking feet and clinked glasses and everyone would have sung "For He's a Jolly Good Fellow". Then Holy God would have bent down to us kindly.

"*I scáth a chéile a mhaireann na daoine.* And you know what that means, don't you? We all live in each other's shadows, we all depend on one another and that's the long and the short of it."

I close my eyes and open them again. Got to get back to Enamel Time, otherwise I won't be able to get all the tenses to meet properly, for that is what this is, a reunion of the tenses, in B Plus Minor, served up for you on a plate.

42

We have driven back to Paris in the rented car at a speed of three months a second and I am dropping Elska off at the apartment on rue Jacob and returning to the Alabama. We didn't kiss, we had rejoined the world of subterfuge and we were friends again. I was keeping an eye on her for a while, that was all. She said she would call me.

It was fully spring and everything was brighter. The dust-filled parts of my room, of my thinking, were suddenly illuminated, like a blessing of some sort. Two days passed and Elska didn't call. I left a message. Finally, the day before Flyte was to return, she called me; she wanted to meet that evening, so we walked down to the river for a drink.

What she had to say hardly surprised me. It was inevitable, really. She had made up her mind. Or thought she had done. And I was strangely unperturbed by it. Was it because I felt so optimistic, because I said to myself that I had had a wonderful time, despite the grating chat in the restaurant? What did I know about love, anyway? Naturally, I had no idea that my very diffidence would be the one thing to keep the affair open, like a book you can briefly forget about and go back to later. Strangest of all was that I felt I had to try to put up a front and appear wounded, but my acting wasn't up to it. I don't know what kind of a mood I was in.

"No, we can't see each other," Elska said, as we stood by the river on the quayside. "Flyte is coming back tomorrow morning and I can't lie to him anymore."

"It's your decision."

"You always say that."

"Well, it is, isn't it?"

"I'm sorry."

"That's the second time you've said sorry. Don't be. We had a good time. You're telling me it's over. So be it! Now let's go and have a drink."

I knew it wasn't over. I imagined Flyte going off to live in New York and me and Elska being together somehow. But we'd have to see about that. Elska and I had a drink. Then she said she had to go. She was upset, I could tell.

"What will happen will be meant to happen, Elska. We'll just have to see what that is. Won't we?"

We parted on the rue Bonaparte and I went off to meet Agostini. He was in a good mood; Agostini is always in a good mood, even when he's spoiling for a fight. He had decided he had met the perfect girl and he was going to give her a lesson in pasta cooking the next day.

"No one can cook anymore," he said to me. "When I told her my speciality was *pasta al forno* she said, '*Cannelloni?*' Imagine! *Cannelloni!* I couldn't believe it."

"So what did you tell her, Agostini?"

"*Cannelloni? Banale!*"

"I quite like *cannelloni*."

"Fine. But it's not one of my specialities. My specialities have a lot more to them than that. No one understands these things. No one."

"No one understands much, Agostini. Cooking *pasta al forno*. Love. We haven't got a clue really."

"Love is a lot easier, Twist, I'm telling you. A lot easier than *pasta al forno.* If you only knew how to cook, you'd understand that. It would make your life a lot easier. You'd be able to fall in love and everything would fit into place perfectly. For what more is there to life than that? Love and *pasta* and a bottle of Il Corvo."

"I don't know, Agostini. I'm more of a fish and chips man myself."

"You're obsessed with fish, Twist. Aren't you?"

"Not cooking it. Catching it. And eating it."

"I'll cook it for you."

"You'll have to find a pretty big *forno* for the tuna me and Mad Joe are going to catch."

"I got money, Twist. I can buy a *forno* as big as you like."

"So, you think this girl you just found is up for it, then?"

"I'll tell you tomorrow."

43

It was May. Marcello wasn't well. I knew he was dying. He had become too tired for all the business of living, he just stayed in his room, in his dressing gown and velvet hat, its tassel falling to his forehead as he moved this way and that in his chair or in bed to try to get himself comfortable.

I spent most of my time in the Alabama because I wanted him to know he could call on me when he needed to. And I began to busy myself with Dad, annotating the biography written by the Englishman and going through papers, letters and unpublished work. I went to the cellar of a friend's apartment, where everything was kept from the old apartment on the rue Monge, and I found boxes filled with material, which I took up to Room 76 to catalogue.

I was motivated to sort out Dad's affairs by the thought that people didn't know even half the truth about him, twenty years after his death, but also by gratitude for earning me all that money – now running out, of course – which had been earned by selling "Heaven and Hell" to the chap in the Crest Hotel. Seeing Marcello fading away in his room, I saw how essential it was for some kind of truth to be known about those who live and die, known or unknown, yet who must be remembered, for otherwise we are all little more than cows in the field, not that there is anything wrong with being a cow in a field necessarily. It's just that if a man spends a lifetime trying to say something, it's better if it's heard correctly and not confused with the trappings and pitfalls of what Smythe would call "poetic existence". In an ideal world, the personality should vanish behind the work, but the world is far from ideal and mostly interested in subliminal pleasures of one sort or another. Gossip, mostly.

What Dad had to say is all in the poems, of course, but he was not old when he died – quite young, in fact, only fifty – and he would have said more and people would have read it and enjoyed it. The proof of that is in the unpublished material, the *inédit*. Some of it was excellent, some of it less so. How to judge it objectively was the problem. I remember what Dad had to say about critics. "There's one of them in America who is always writing about the poems. It appears he likes them but doesn't care to admit it. Grudging and tortured, he goes at them with a scalpel, shaving them here and there, when what he really needs is a felling axe. They're not precious things, the poems, they're not supposed to be, they are robust and made to last."

Some evenings, I would read out Dad's *inédits* to Marcello, as he lay there, sipping his whisky and smoking a cigarette or a cheroot.

"It's good," he would say. "But I don't think he would have thought so. After all, there is a reason he published some things and not others, is there not?"

"It's hard to say, isn't it, Marcello? There are different categories. Ones he liked from the early days which he might have forgotten about, ones he didn't like and didn't want published, later ones he wanted to have published, later ones that weren't finished."

"You have an unenviable task, Twist."

"I should discuss it with the other half. Things have changed now. I wonder what Dad would have thought about writing a pop song."

"He'd be amused by it."

"Yes, he was always making jokes about being modern. He thought that, as far as writing and art was concerned, the Twentieth Century had come as a terrible shock to the English and that they never quite came to terms with it. But he always published his English stuff in London, rather than Dublin or New York."

"Your father was very kind, Seamus. I know he would have been very pleased that you sold his poem for a pop song so that you could spend time sorting out his things and having a good time occasionally."

"Yes, he was kind. A tough act to follow."

"All good acts are tough acts to follow. But you don't always have to follow them, you know. The worst is coming on after a good comedian. The best is after a bad one. You're a poet, Twist. You're like your father. Even if you don't write. You don't need to."

"I've wasted a lot. Time, mostly."

"It's not too late to do things. You're young. How old are you?"

"We're forty in July."

"Look at me. I'm over twice your age. And I have done nothing. At least, I have nothing to show for it. Save for the odd photograph or press clipping. And a couple of funny hats."

"You don't need anything to show who you are, Marcello. You're fine the way you are. Just fine."

"Thanks, Twist. Now read me another poem. We talk too much."

I read him a poem. It was very late, very early, four or five in the morning. I went downstairs to reception and sat with Régis. We watched the men across the street setting up the rotisserie outside the butcher's.

"Every day, the same ritual," said Régis.

They were moving a wheeled counter onto the pavement and placing a cut-out wooden duck beside it, while a plastic heart, a memento from last Valentine's Day, still swung hopefully from the awning.

"Say it with a chicken."

"Yes, same ritual, same chickens, all of them uneatable." Régis rolled a cigarette and pointed to the key box behind him. "See that, Seamus? Max bought it years ago, when the Alabama had three floors and forty rooms. He got it in the flea market. But there was room for seventy-six keys. So he built another three floors to accommodate them. I like that story."

"So do I, Régis. Max was a man with a purpose. He made the finest hotel in all of Paris. Not a television in sight and an atmosphere born of love and circumspection."

For the first time in nearly a year I wasn't thinking about Elska.

44

One morning, I came across a letter Dad wrote to the mammy: "I always dreamed of you and only you, from the first, you were the one and the one and only and I would [I couldn't decipher this word, it was crossed out, amended and then spilled upon] to touch and hold you or even just a part of you, a strand of hair as it falls in the emerald breeze of your eyes, a finger of your hand as it rests upon my lip to silence me.

"There is here a breeze of sorts but it and nothing like it is real without you to make it real for me, I flop and flounder alone without you and my steps are a march through muddy solitude. I long for that place, high up and dry as a biscuit, home to your smile and kisses and, when I see you again, I will be good and loving and try not to get pissed like the last time.

"How are the boys, all three of them, our favourites? What happened to the knee of Seamus and the heart of Myles, for he seemed a trifle *triste* as I fell through the back door of happiness into this unwholesome trip in order to answer questions and make money? Please find enclosed some baksheesh. I love you as of forever, your everloving husband ..."

I put it with the others, neatly folded, and determined that no one else should read it for the time being. It was an early letter, during Dad's first visit to America to do lecturing, and there was a sincerity to it that took my breath away; it illuminated my parents for me, making me think of them as lovers and not parents at all for a moment, Dad's reference to us feeling rather abstract and strangely out of place, adding another dimension to his heart, as if it had been held up to me in a sharper light. And what a heart he had too.

I can't remember exactly how I hurt my knee but I do recall the other half being at home with flu and me being at school and he informing the mammy that I had injured it. The mammy came to pick us up, Myles and me, and nearly fainted when she saw what the other half had seen, from afar. So it was that she always believed pain to be the surest wire of telepathy and the longest. She was right, for she had the telepathy and could usually tell what was what from a distance, especially if one of us happened to be in trouble. The day Myles got killed she tripped on the bottom stair in the apartment building and turned to me: "Something's not right this day, Seamus, and I don't like it."

These letters and unpublished works had not been shown to the biographer and I determined to keep them sealed until such time as they could be used correctly. I felt some sympathy for the English chap. He hadn't seen all the material so how could I blame him for not getting it all right? But the letters were all the same, simple love letters, that's all. The mammy was all Dad ever wanted or needed. How fine that is! I look back, from the duddlededum of the train in England, into my past, to countless fleeting loves, through the infatuation with Elska, and I long for that simplicity of desire, for I truly believe that is what it was for Dad and for the mammy too.

I had not really thought of Elska, so busy had I been with Dad's ghost and the closing days of Marcello, but as I read the letters I was drawn back to her through Dad's honest vision of love and his constancy of desire and, as I did so, I projected myself into a sublime love which was a renewed desire for Elska. She was always part fantasy, part real, there was always a dream of sorts to sustain it, and Dad's tender words of love inspired my longing for her.

I would pass by Marcello's room two or three times a day. Once I asked him: "Dad only loved the mammy, didn't he, Marcello? From the first. Just as you only had the one."

"That's right, Seamus. I never saw him flirt or go with another woman and I knew him from his first years here, when he came from Dublin with your mother in the Fifties."

"Because he wasn't interested?"

"He loved women. He wrote about them a lot. You know that. But it was always your mother he wrote about."

It was mid-June. Marcello was getting more and more tired and I did not know how long he would last. I wanted him to die there, in his room, and not have to go to some hospital, where death is robbed of peace and dignity and becomes instead a sort of logistical problem. Marcello deserved dignity in his dying.

"Pour me a cup of whisky, will you, Seamus, and read me a poem?"

I read him the poem in which Dad unravels the sea, wave by wave, and then he folds all the waves up on the seabed so that the fish can sleep and dream. It was a poem Dad used to read to us when we were little. I think he must have written it for us. It was a poem for children, perhaps, and a poem for the old, the first and third ages, who know so much more than the others. The fish dream up the sea and, when they awaken, they are swimming about again, as if nothing had ever happened. But they have learned what sleep is and they long for more.

"You can rest a while later
Sweet fishes of the sea,
When the lines are all in
And the mammy's set the tea."

Marcello loved this poem. He gave a broad smile when I'd finished reading it, took a drag of his cigarette and a swig of whisky and stubbed his cigarette out in the ashtray by his bed. Then he closed his eyes and died. The smoke from his half-extinguished cigarette rose slowly up to the ceiling and a tear fell from my cheek.

"Well done, Marcello. Living's easy. But a good death, that takes talent."

45

A few days before he died, Marcello gave me the scrap-book filled with bits of poems Dad had written in Room 7 and told me to show it to the other half.

Dad would write on anything he found, sometimes in the street – paper, card, parking ticket – and he often used words from signs, snatches of conversation, writing them out in different ways and creating what he called his "Ambulations". He never quite knew which language to write in first so he would just write in the first language that came to him. Often, these poems would become a code to his frustration and desire, to the struggle between technique and imagination, his twinned tormentors; he would tear up the paper and stick the pieces back together again in a furious attempt to contrast sound and meaning. I remember being dispatched to the Rally to summon him home for his tea; he would be in a corner with mounds of paper and bottles in front of him.

"Where's that damned *morceau*! I lost the *extrait*! Find it, lad!"

"I don't know what it looks like!"

"Just pick anything up, Seamus, it's all the same difference. Bit of chance now and then won't hurt the picture."

I would scramble around on the floor and find the edge of a beer mat or the cellophane strip from a cigarette wrapper, anything I could lay my hands on.

"Perfect, lad!" he would say, patting me on the back. "Perfect! Get yourself a drink!"

I was running out of money. It happens. I spent my last thousand francs on Marcello's funeral. Agostini paid the rest. He'd taken Marcello's portrait and he knew how important he was to me. The wake was a good bash. We buried Marcello in Père Lachaise and then went over to the Rally and drank up and down until we'd had enough.

Wolf and Régis told me I could stay on a while if I wanted, as Room 7 was not being used. So I moved downstairs. It was the end of June and I would lie on the bed, thinking of Dad and looking through the scrap-book. On the first page was an Ambulation which intrigued me more than the others. I tried to make sense of it as I lay there and I saw that it reappeared, in different guises, elsewhere in the book:

HERTRIP
CHERIERIP
HERTRIPE
CHERIERIPE
HERIERIPERIE
HERIETRIP
HERIETRIPER

Or:

CHE	RIE	T	RIPE
RIPE	RIE		
TRIP	ER		
I			
RIP			
CHE	RIE	TRI	PERIE
I			

BOUCHE   T   RIP

Dad was probably just playing with ideas, but he considered all his work to have the same value and he would devote as much time to a *Métro* ticket Ambulation as he might to a saga of fifty pages. "It's all a search for something," he would say. "Thing is to know when you've found it."

I felt the time filling, bursting almost, and I knew I would soon be leaving. I wasn't sure what to do about my finances, or lack of them. Agostini took me out and said he would help.

"I want to go to London, Agostini. I haven't seen the other half for over a year. We never need to see each other, but we need to see each other now. Marcello is dead, we'll be forty on 12 July and I plan on going over to Long Island afterwards to catch that tuna. I can always get work on a boat or sell a poem to the chap with the ponytail."

"That's a good plan, Twist. But I'll miss you. I'll give you money. I have lots of it and I don't need so much."

"Thanks, Agostini. Why don't I sell you something?"

"You don't have to do that."

"I know. But it would make me feel better."

"Listen, I don't want to buy one of your father's poems. I don't think poems are something I could ever buy. A book, maybe. But then I never buy books either. I don't really care for words."

"I know, Agostini. I know. I was thinking of something else. Something more practical."

"Like what?"

"Like a .357 Magnum."

"Great. I've always wanted one of those."

"You have?"

"I can give it to my uncle for Christmas or something."

"Yeah. Make a nice present, wouldn't it? You'll need some bullets, though. I'll send you some from the States. What do you want? Holopoint? They're the best, apparently."

"Holopoint's fine, Twist."

46

And Elska?

After selling Agostini the Magnum, I was lying in my room one evening, suddenly feeling at peace with myself. Dad used to call it the eye of the storm; he was talking about his work, he said it was the only time he could be calm and that it only came through the writing. I don't know how I find it. It just happens, like the weather, like a tornado.

I had reason to feel good, though. I had a plan. Agostini had helped me out again, Moraes was due back in town the next day, a year had passed and there was bound to be another party or other to go to. I could feel a circle turning, my heart carried with it onto some new horizon.

I had called Mad Joe to tell him I was coming over in a week or so and I had called the other half to plan the birthday lunch. Marcello had died well and Paris was in a heatwave. And I love nothing more than the heat, my blood warms up and I feel alive and I can't get enough of it, it's like being stuck thirty miles out on a flat sea with Mad Joe at the helm and an ice-cold beer in my hand, and you can't possibly beat that, can you?

There was a knock on the door. I opened it. It was Elska, standing there, on the threshold.

"Well, come in."

She fell into my arms and we sat on the bed, holding hands, like teenagers.

"What's up?"

"I miss you."

"I miss you too."

"I heard about your friend, Marcello. Agostini told me. I knew you'd be sad."

"Of course. Can't be much else when you say good-bye to someone but for ever. He was old. And he died with a brass cup of whisky in his hand. I'm proud of him."

"Yes."

"How are you, Elska?"

"OK."

"Flyte?"

"OK too."

"You know what Hemingway said about fishing, don't you, Elska? He said that for the first five minutes, you've hooked the marlin and that, for the rest of the time, the marlin has hooked you."

"I don't know much about fishing, Twist."

"Neither do I. But I'm learning."

"I thought you were in the room at the top, with the balcony."

"I moved into Dad's old room. I'm not supposed to be following in the steps. But I'm not doing a very good job, am I?"

"There's no harm in that."

"Do you think if I were different it would be better between us? Maybe I should become silent and mysterious. You know, the brooding type. I was thinking about that, the other day. I even tried doing it. It's easy in the room because there's no one to talk to. But I managed to keep it up for at least ten minutes in the Armistice, even though everyone was trying to talk to me."

"Ten minutes? Is that a record, Twist?"

"Must be."

I poured us a drink. Then I kissed her. We didn't talk. We just took our clothes off and got into the single bed together. We made love and it was perfect, just as it always was. Afterwards, Elska looked at the scrap-book on the bedside table and turned to me.

"What's that?" she said, picking it up and opening the cover to page one and the first Tripe Ambulation:

I
RIP
TRIP
RIPE
TRIPE
TRIPERIE

"I can't for the life of me think where Dad found that one. I've been pondering it. Must have made it up on a dark night."

We were lying in each other's arms. It was late. And still hot. A neon sign had begun to glow, flickeringly, on the wall opposite. It was the sign for the wine shop and it spread a beautiful, almost divine blue across the street towards us, bathing our naked bodies in a shadowless pool of light.

Elska stared out with me, through the open window.

"There it is, Twist."

"What?"

"Your father's poem."

She was right. In faded lettering affixed to the wall, yet still visible above the neon in pale green paint, was Dad's sign, and it wavered left and right as the curtains between the open window were pushed an inch or so either side by a sudden breeze, its syllables alternating, like a verse to be declaimed in different ways according to accent and tongue, the English TRIP, the English/French TRIPE, followed by the English RIPE and so on, in a seemingly endless lullaby of variables:

BOUCHERIE TRIPERIE

"I think Dad once began a book called *Tripe*," I said, holding Elska in my arms. "Or planned to. Perhaps it was a joke."

"Why?"

"Well, in French it means just what it is: tripe. But, in English, it also means rubbish. Just think of all the hours he spent in this room, playing with that simple idea!"

"We don't have so much time. I'm supposed to be at a movie."

"We have all the time we need, Elska. The whole thing is an illusion, anyway, you should know that by now. The night is eternal and a life flashes before your eyes, like a sign."

"I'm learning, Twist."

"Good. Kiss me, then. You can get a lot into a movie."

47

We made love again and we fell asleep, Elska's head on my shoulder, our dreams colliding in the narrow bed, a barrelful of thick, white tripe, a heaving sea, a spot at the edge of the woods by a lake.

When I awoke, Elska was standing by the basin in a corner of the room, picking her clothes up from the floor. I lit a cigarette and watched her dress.

"What am I going to say?" she muttered.

"Tell him you fell asleep."

"Don't be silly."

"Yeah, you fell asleep. It was a long movie. There was a fire in the cinema. Then an earthquake. Then a tsunami. You got on the wrong bus which broke down. There was a tuna tail-back on rue du 12 juillet."

She smiled, the moment stilled. I stroked her hair and kissed her: "Tell him you're having an affair. Everyone has affairs in Paris. He'll understand."

She laughed. "I think I'll settle for the long movie."

I will freeze this scene for ever, longer if necessary. I am stealing it, even now, from the precious, sapphire light of Room 7, thinking of it as the last time, *post scriptum* to a great love. I am able to record it indelibly, like a painting, or a photograph with all the edges neatly in place, I have hung it up upon the far wall of my mind and gone out and bought a fancy brass lamp to stick over it.

I have no idea what she is thinking as she dresses (when did I ever know what she was thinking?), apart from her fear of being so late home and having to explain herself to Mr Gatsby. She was as distant from me then as she is now, but the knowledge that this is the last time lends the scene an unbearable intensity she must surely be sharing with me as the train rattles on north through fields dotted with sheep, hops and hedges. Oh, Elska! I know what love is! Please believe me!

She stood before me. I had found her shoe under the bed and I handed it to her, dismally, and kissed her. She broke away from me and said she had to run and she was gone, into the night. And I lay back on the bed and inhaled her scent, sweet noting, sweet nothing, of her absence.

I couldn't sleep. I sat at the small table by the window and reread the scrap-book, all the while thinking of Elska climbing the stairs to the apartment on rue Jacob, slipping her key into the lock and tiptoeing along the hall. She drops her bag onto the sofa, she goes over to the mantelpiece, glances at herself in the mirror, then at the absurd, bronze pachyderms, their opened mouths turned in a knowing smile. The elephants, those damned elephants, sticking their trunks into everything, memorizing every snippet, storing it all up for some later date to be used against us!

She nods in resignation, pours herself a glass of port and lies back on the sofa, too nervous to slip into bed next to her neatly folded husband. She has to be thinking of me, sitting in Room 7; yes, she *is* thinking of me, we're heading away from this safari-land of dinners and movies and elephants that never go anywhere but just stand half-dead on the mantel, snorting. Give me a lion any day of the week; better still, a tiger, a pair of tigers, with hoops lit by a slick, blackening flame for them to jump through.

48

Moraes arrived in town. And I found myself having a drink with Agostini in the Rally, exactly as I had done twelve months earlier, discussing a party.

"Are Flyte and Elska going to be there?" I asked him.

"I'm not sure."

"When did you speak to them?"

"This morning, late. Flyte was upset about something. I've never heard him like that before."

"What do you mean, 'upset'?"

"I don't know. It was his voice."

"Is he OK?"

"I think so. They're going to New York. To live. You know that, don't you?"

"What's wrong with Paris all of a sudden? Not modern enough?"

"There's more to it than that. Must be."

"Who can say? I never really knew Flyte."

"I thought you were friends."

"Sure. But you don't always know your friends, do you? No matter how much time you spend with them. What about Elska?" I asked. "What does she think about moving to New York?"

"It's a while since I spoke to her, Twist."

I wanted to tell Agostini about it all. Surely he would

understand Elska should be with me and not Flyte. It was so obvious to me. But I didn't trust myself, I knew I was probably deluded, however certain I was. And I still clung to the idea he would disapprove.

We started to walk over the river to the party. Then Agostini stopped me in my tracks. "I'm not sure I want to go."

"Why ever not?"

"Well, there's someone I'd rather not see."

"Who's that?" I was intrigued. Agostini had never talked to me like this before.

"You remember that Dutch girl, Kajfa?"

"Sure I do."

"We had an affair."

"You did? Well done, Agostini. She was great."

"It ended badly. She might be at the party and I don't want to see her."

"Don't worry. If you want to go to the party, you go to the party. Tell me about it. I need to know."

"It was in the spring. Kajfa was working on a fashion shoot we did in Morocco. You know how it is."

"I can imagine. Sunshine. Pretty girl. Sand everywhere. Drinks. Hotel with a fountain in it."

"It didn't last long. We saw each other in Paris and she found out about me and the Russian girl. You remember the Russian girl?"

"I think so."

"Of course you do. She came from Siberia. Somewhere like that. Anyway, we had this big fight, Kajfa and me. She was so angry. *Cazzo!* It was my place. She found the girl's lipstick. And that's when it all came out. By the bed there. With the lipstick of the Russian."

"You're a terrible story-teller, Agostini. Good job you stick to taking pictures."

"She got hold of one of my tripods and banged me over the head with it. Imagine that! The shame of it! And she was screaming. She said she was sick of being used by all of us. 'All of us?' I asked. 'Yeah. You and Flyte,' she said, shouting and everything."

"Flyte?"

"Turns out Flyte was having an affair with her. For quite a while."

"For how long? When did it start?"

"Must have been last summer. It was certainly going on at the time of that dinner party with the Frenchman who didn't like Hollywood."

I was in shock. I needed a drink. My mind went back to those ridiculous dinners. So that was it! I knew something was up and I could see, as clear as day, Flyte looking at Kajfa intently across that oval table on rue Jacob, or facing me across his desk, his mind all chewed up with guilt and deception. The mere fact that the two of them avoided each other so studiously should have told me something.

I had been set up. Flyte wanted us to have an affair because he was having an affair with Kajfa. It was how his mind worked. He couldn't handle Elska, so he turned to someone else. It had to be a friend, didn't it? The funny part was that he was organized and proper even when he was betraying someone. His Calvinist upbringing meant he had to check the scales and balances of it all, to ease his conscience, to transform everything into something abstract; a game, or the plot of some story or other with a beginning and a middle and an ending all worked out beforehand.

"Did Elska ever find out?"

"Of course not. I told Kajfa that if she told anyone else about it I'd come after her."

"Are you sure?"

"Of course. Don't tell anyone, Twist. Promise!"

"I promise."

"Otherwise I'll come after you."

"You wouldn't come after me, Agostini."

"Of course I wouldn't. Pretty strange tale, though. Don't you think?"

"I've heard stranger. But not much."

We arrived at the apartment and knocked on the door. Everyone was there, like last time, save Moraes, who would come later. I had a Scotch and tried to calm myself down. I was actually disgusted. But I didn't show it. I didn't want to give anything away. I was also elated. This all meant something important. Flyte was a cad too. But a worse one. He'd been reading too many books when he should have been writing them. And me? I had all the leverage I needed to win Elska. If I wanted. That was the rub.

"This is the good life, Twist," Agostini said, clinking my glass.

"That's right, Agostini. With all the edges in place."

We chatted to friends and acquaintances and I looked out for Flyte and Elska, my mind turning through all the events of the past year, piecing it all together and trying to make sense of it, all the while altering my perception of the man I had assumed lacked sufficient passion to act out his fantasies. How wrong can anyone be?

They never came, neither Flyte nor Elska. Nor Kajfa. Of course they didn't. They knew we'd be there. When Moraes arrived I embraced him; we got a drink and went off to a corner, apart from the crowd.

"So, Twist. What's up?"

"Not much."

"What have you been doing?"

"I was a gangster in a film. I went through Dad's work.

Marcello died. I fell in love."

"Elska?"

"Yes. Elska."

"Thought so. She's a beautiful woman. But I warned you, didn't I?"

"Yes, you warned me. What is a *passarinho*, anyway?"

"You should know. A bird."

"I get it. We have a less explicit way of saying the same thing."

"You would. You're English."

"Irish, Moraes."

"Irish. *O passarinho que come pedra sabe o cu que tem.* The bird who eats the stone knows the size of his arsehole. Just an expression, Twist. Just an expression."

"That's right. But I don't eat stones. And I'm not a bird. I can't stand heights."

"So, you're all right, then. It doesn't apply to you. You're free."

"Well, I still bit off more than I could chew this time. Can't argue with that."

"Good fun, though, isn't it? I mean, what are you going to do? Take life in little mouthfuls?"

"No fear of that, Moraes."

49

Agostini wanted to leave the party, so I bade farewell to Moraes and we left and walked out into Paris. We strolled back over to the Left Bank and had a drink at the Armistice.

"It is a strange story, Agostini. Are you sure about it?"

"Of course I'm sure."

I felt a cheat. Unless I told Agostini about Elska now it would be unfair. And Agostini was my friend. This was serious business. He had told me everything. Now it was my turn. I'd have to accept the consequences.

"Well, I'll tell you a story." And I told him all about me and Elska. From start to finish. He looked at me and nodded. And waited a while before answering.

"I know, Twist. I know. It's obvious. You can't hide anything from me."

"You knew all along?"

"Of course. And when you told me you were in love with a woman who was married, it didn't take much for me to guess who it might be."

"The strange thing is I'll never know Flyte's real motives. He asked me to check up on Elska and he admitted afterwards he thought she might have been having an affair. He knew I was attracted to her. Perhaps it was his own idea of revenge of some sort. The irony is she wasn't having an affair when he thought she was. In a way the whole plot is way off the mark. Load of old tripe, really."

"Tripe?"

"Well, not tripe. I can't call it anything. Because I don't know what the truth is. I don't suppose anyone does." I felt light-hearted then and curiously indifferent. "You haven't told anyone, have you?" I added.

"Who do you think I am?" Agostini was suddenly angry. I had never seen him like that before. Angry with me, that is. "I only told you about Kajfa and me and Flyte because I knew it would affect you. Otherwise I wouldn't have. There was no love between us, between me and Kajfa. And I can't see much love, much real love, between Elska and Flyte. But I can see it between Elska and you. Strange, I was lecturing you from the start about love and yet you are the one to have found it. Is that why I'm angry?"

"You'll find someone, Agostini. You always do. But you'll find the real one, the one who will make you happy and make you pasta *al forno* in Naples. You'll have a tableful of children and they will all be just like you, upright, passionate, worldly wise."

"Thanks, Twist. Have a drink. You're leaving tomorrow. And I'll miss you."

"I'll miss you too."

We chatted for a while about different things and then we said good-bye.

"Here, take this," he said, slipping a small envelope into my top pocket.

"What is it? You gave me some money already."

"It's some cocaine. It'll help you tomorrow for your trip. Great way to pick up a girl too. They like that."

"I don't want to pick up a girl, Agostini. I just want to have lunch with my other half."

"What you want and what you get are two different things. Besides, it's your birthday. You never know what'll happen, do you?"

I watched him disappear around the corner and I went back to the Alabama. It was late. I packed up my things, all I ever need, in two suitcases. My clothes, two suits, half a dozen shirts, two pairs of shoes and my fishing clothes – shorts, trainers, leatherpeaked cap – in one case. Books in the other: the travelling library, Dad, Yeats, Papini, Behan, Borges, O'Brien, Bontempelli and a few others, including *Teach Yourself Finnish* and *Tuna: The Big One* by someone called Pringle. Then I lay down for a few hours, awaiting the moment when I would get up and go, leave the Alabama for ever, which it never is, even though it feels like it sometimes. It was then that I thought up the birthday poem for the other half, not as I was leaving but as I lay there, waiting to leave. It was a good time to make up a poem, just about the best, when the dawn comes and asks questions of you.

At eight-thirty, the telephone rang. It was Elska.

"I have to see you," she said. "Before you go."

"Come over."

"No. A café."

We met in the café on place St Sulpice. *Café crème, pain au chocolat*, Calvados. Elska had an *express*.

"What time's you train?"

"Quarter past ten. Ten nineteen to be exact."

"We haven't got long."

"When did we ever? You weren't at the party last night. What happened? Was it difficult?"

"Flyte got home at five in the morning. I was waiting for him. He was drunk. He said he'd been out with the boys. When does he ever go out with the boys?"

"I don't know."

"We had a row. It just started all on its own. I was probably angry because I was so nervous about sleeping at the Alabama and being late and him finding out. But I could tell there was something. I know him inside out. He's like a book. A thin book."

"Is he?" I felt sad for her. She thought she knew him.

"Yes. I have known he has been having an affair for ages, but I refused to accept it."

"And has he?"

"Yes."

"Who with?"

"Guess? Well, it's Kajfa. I never liked her."

"I thought she was OK."

"So did I. At first."

"Where is she now then?"

"She's here. Somewhere."

"So he admitted it?"

"I forced it out of him. I always thought you were the one living in a fantasy. But I hadn't counted on Flyte. He broke down in front of me. He said he had tried to love me but he couldn't. He said no one could ever love me. What kind of an excuse is that?"

"He's wrong. Did you tell him about us?"

"No."

"Good. He'll find out one day. But it'll be too late. We'll be in Metsalumpy by then and the infants will already have become prize fishermen."

"Stop it, Twist. This is not a joke."

"I'm not joking, Elska."

I looked at my watch, at the Omega that didn't work. But I knew I would have to run, otherwise I'd miss the train. "So what next?"

"Why do I always have to make the decisions, Twist?"

"No reason. But I've got to go. Got a fish to catch."

"Flyte's going to New York. To live."

"And you?"

"I'm going to stay here for a while. Then I'll see. I'm tired. I want to go home."

"Home? Do we know where that is?"

"Perhaps I'll find out. Could be Metsalämpi, after all. Not the one in Finland. Perhaps another one, somewhere else. And you?"

"I'm just going to take things one lunch at a time." I smiled and downed the Calvados. "I've got to go, Elska. It's been a rough ride lately, for both of us."

She nodded. Then she leaned forward and looked right through me. "You're hopeless, Twist. Hopeless. You want nothing, yet you consume so much. You consumed me. And now you're escaping. You will always be lurching from one thing to the next, living off the present as if everything were a gift. You think you have nothing to lose. But you're wrong."

"Maybe. Or maybe we just don't know one another. Yet." I dropped some money on the table. "You know Keats always put on his best suit before writing a poem. Why do you think he did that?"

"I don't know."

"Neither do I. But maybe it was because he felt if you were going to do something, it was better to do it properly."

She looked up at me and I kissed her on the cheek. "Well, I'm off to catch myself a fish. I'm going to do something that means something. Something real and proper and tangible. Then I'll come back and if you want me and I want you we'll go to Metsalumpy and breed."

"That's right, Twist. It's your turn to make the decisions, after all."

With that, I marched out of the café and went back to the Alabama to get my bags.

50

We're a long way from 300 now. From the noughts.

Or I'll do nothing with them. I'll ignore them, allow them to drift in the air around me, leave them as words slipping in one ear, out the other. Three hundred.

We're entering the outskirts, the underskirts, of London, great mass of brick and sky and platforms for waiting. I haven't seen the girl, she's not smoking somewhere with the man without a name. I've got one page left in the book for writing without anything written on it and I'm thinking of a new list of things.

Bricks.

Lucky Light.

Sky.

Last Martell miniature.

Writing.

Dad.

The Tripe Ambulation.

Elska.

Flyte.

Agostini.

Kajfa.

Girl.

Condom.

Gumboots.

Sea.

Mad Joe.

Tuna.

Chips.

Other half.

Elska.

It never ends, the mind turns, the body needs, the heart sinks, the belly aches, and amidst it all is this word-by-word poem which is a list of living and longing which would surely go on for ever if there was enough paper for it. But we're running out of pulp and I have to pinpoint everything before it's too late, some variable fixed for the purpose of investment in the project. Let's just say that Flyte was insecure, Elska was curious, Kajfa was an opportunist. And I was the fall guy.

The train, this sleek and handsome beast, shaped for speed, turns a curve into more of London and still more, I can see its engines and carriages now ahead of me, it seems so odd that I am actually a part of it, this longest of things ever invented which has carried me from Paris, it's pulling into Waterloo now, I can feel the brakes, the platform is appearing and still we glide into the station, more brakes and finally, but only finally, do we stop dead.

I am walking up to the door, I have closed the book but am still writing in my head for later, I have got hold of my twin cases, one for books, one for clothes, the door is opening and I am out and walking briskly away from it all, down a ramp and through passport control, dropping one case, pulling out my passport, no, I'm just visiting, *de passage*, sir, then I'm through some doors which open automatically, at the head of the taxi queue and now in the cab with the folding seats, we're moving through traffic, over the Thames, Father Thames, past

Parliament, into the park, "*the pelicans get more in their beaks than their bellycans*", the Mall, right, left, right, Piccadilly and parking at Swallows', that's a fiver, I open the door of the restaurant, dump the bags, adjust my tie, take a deep breath and walk into the dining room, the other half is standing up, Sandra has a warm smile, she gives me a hug, nods to the barman who starts pouring the Guinness into the pewter tankard as the other half comes towards me, shakes my hand and gives me a slap on the back, we're sitting down now and, as we do so, Sandra deposits the tankard before me, I raise it into the air, the other half raises his and, as the two tankards meet, it is now, right now, that I deliver the birthday poem, to the other half but also to all and sundry and to the sleepless Gods of Life, Death, Comfort and Stability, to be followed by a round of applause and the sudden freezing of the frame on two faces, in profile, froth of foaming Liffey on the tip of twin-twitching noses:

Per l'altro mezzo
Un proprio gemello
Per "lui" chi è "io"
Un' ombra davvero!

Well, I was hardly going to do nothing with them. With the noughts. Now was I?

Paris and London
17 February 1999

AFTERWORD

Twist was completed in 1999 at a time when the London terminus for the Eurostar was not a saint but a battle, and when it was permissible to smoke in selected carriages (I am assuming any regulations with regard to sexual intercourse are unchanged). The "Walkman" and "box camera" are also things of the past, of course, along with French francs, even if fax machines and telephone cards are still used occasionally. The distance in real time afforded by Eurostar was three hours and not the two hours and twenty minutes as of writing. The eponymous hero would have had to scribble in his notebook even faster in 2010 as a result. If time passes more quickly now, it is usually kinder to fictional characters, although people tend to "live in each other's shadows", whether real or invented by me. As for the period in question, it may be strange to think of the Nineties as part of an old world but the expression *fin-de-siècle* inevitably adds dust to one's thoughts. Perhaps a lost innocence can be conjured up when thinking pre-9/11; or, indeed, decadence, a wholly romantic view of things and people, as refracted through the prism of a crystal tumbler, subsequently shattered, of course, by so many alarm bells? If so, why not? Escapism takes many forms, not all of them practical, although you can't beat a bullet train. The novel itself could be loosely regarded as being the third part of a trilogy – its antecedents being *Still-Life With Books* (1993) and *Fear* (1998) – inasmuch as Paris is the real protagonist, above and beyond all earthly, unearthly concerns.

Simon Lane,
Rio de Janeiro, 24 June 2010

ABOUT THE AUTHOR

SIMON LANE was born in England. After graduating from art school in London in 1979, he lived successively in Berlin, Milan, New York and Paris, before settling in Rio de Janeiro in 2001. His poetry, short stories, essays and drawings have appeared in publications throughout Europe and the United States. He has also worked in film, television and radio, as a writer and as an actor. Lane is the author  of four novels, *Le Veilleur, Still-life with Books, Fear, Boca a Boca* and a collection of stories, *The Real Illusion.*

Author photograph by Barbara Leary

www.ingramcontent.com/pod-product-compliance
Lightning Source LLC
Chambersburg PA
CBHW050518260626
47157CB00004B/1381